NO WAR

STUFF ABOUT GOD,

ANYMORE

First published in the United States in 2009 by
ATNA INK
3750-B Calle de Ricardo
Palm Springs, CA 92264

Library of Congress Holdings Information:
LC Control No.: 2009920522
Ferguson, Paul [author]
No War Stuff About God, Anymore [title]
   an autobiography in short fiction
[fiction, literature, collections, short-stories]
compiled & edited by J. Michael Bell.
288p. 13.97 x 21.59 cm.

ISBN   9780966080209

NO WAR STUFF ABOUT GOD, ANYMORE

Paul Ferguson

ATNA INK

Palm Springs
2009

A lie can travel halfway around the world while the truth is still putting on its shoes.

(attributed) Mark Twain, (1835 – 1910)

US humorist, short story author, & wit

To:

Drifters, dreamers & misfits.

Paul Ferguson

BAREFOOT

I know this guy. He's been dead over twenty-five years now and I still often think about fishing with him. He taught me how to catch shiners. And it's true they're as much fun as casting for bass. So, if you've ever been interested in how to do it, this story tells you?

9

"Barefoot"

I don't know when we first started calling him 'Barefoot'. It's the sort of thing folks around here do when a fellow quits wearing shoes. A few years back his wife Annie died and he turned the farm over to his boy and his wife and moved out to the old cabin along the river. He seems happy enough, except it's a mile walk across country through the woods to church Sundays, but his legs are still good, and he gets to fish undisturbed, which is how he likes it.

You're not likely to see much of him. He's a little fellow, a bit bent across the shoulders and back, an old, slouched, gray felt hat on his bald head, and he'll be wearing a faded denim work-shirt with worn out bib-overalls; generally, he'll have the pant legs rolled up to his knees and he'll be wet, wading in the river, but don't let his looks fool you. Barefoot ain't no scrofulous bum. He looks after himself.

Most mornings he's out of bed early and through the cabin door and off the porch with the mist still heavy, curling among the pines and hardwoods along the bank and laying low and gray like smoke on the river. It's real quiet then, the air just warming, the water still cold, and him the only thing moving with the mist. He's after trout before the sun rises and the river warms and the trout bed down out of the day's heat.

Barefoot likes nothing better for breakfast than a pound or so of fresh caught trout fillet, salted, fried in butter on that old, woodstove in an old, well-seasoned, cast iron skillet – the whole process taking about ten minutes and worth every bite of it.

Barefoot knows this river, every rock and rill, the sandbars and deep holes, all the way from the shoals above the cabin down to Frogs Bend. That's about eight to ten miles. The waters are full of trout and small mouth bass and crappie. They make for good fishing and fine eating. If you ever had a mess of fried crappie with strong sweet tea and fried cornbread, you'll know what I mean.

I prefer crappie, but Barefoot likes angling. He says he's giving the bass a sporting chance. By mid-morning he'll be out catching shiners. He uses a light pole rigged with thread tied to a safety pin baited with pieces of worm. He casts for minnows and it is almost as much fun as catching the big ones. The bass like shiners. He can fill a bucket with them in a couple of hours. The big bass bite better in the late afternoon, towards evening. You feel that first freshening breeze of the night and can almost smell them. Barefoot has taken some big seven and eight pound bass on light tackle. He cooks them same as trout, quick in butter, salting them, sizzling in the skillet.

Of course, there are lots of catfish in the river, and Barefoot has a trotline or two out for them and spoonbills. He runs the lines at night.

You wouldn't think he could, the way that wooden rowboat of his leaks. He has to keep bailing to stay afloat, but that ain't no problem for him. He sells the catfish or carries them to the boy and his wife to help them out. They make more money on crops than Barefoot ever did. The boy buys a new pickup truck every year, but claims he is broke and times are hard. He doesn't know about hard times, what they can really mean, and that seems alright with Barefoot. He says everything today is easier, even hard times, and you can't blame folks for what they don't know.

The boy's son is ten years-old. Barefoot's grandson. He is as much in love with the river and fishing as Barefoot himself, and is the devil for running off from home and showing up to fish with his granddad. Just seeing them together in the early morning, wading the shoals, casting their lines in the mist, makes you feel good, maybe, even a little sad, but also kind of hopeful. You can't help but smile while knowing it's not something you see much of anymore. You know too, what it must mean to Barefoot. These are special days for him. You might say everyday is special for Barefoot. I kind of envy him.

Paul Ferguson

THE BEGINNING

Here's a mix – UFO's, jail, and the bible. The UFO's are taken from my own experience in 1956, in Stillwell, IL, when two ships decided to hover over our farmhouse and take a look at us. Why were they interested? Who knows? Still, they hung above the yard where we were all gathered to look up at them. My brother, John, who died at thirty-eight of heart disease, once told his son, Jon-Jon, that he expected them to come back and give him the cure for his heart. They didn't. Or did they?

The Beginning

"Yeah, there are UFO's," I said, overhearing the speculations of four guys sitting together against the building's yellow brick wall, their pale faces made paler by the hot overhead sun reflecting off the wall, and from the bright orange of their jail jumpsuits, matching my own.

I squatted down among them without waiting for an invitation. "If I had never seen a UFO," I said, looking from one sweaty face to another, "I wouldn't be in jail."

The guy on my near right, evidently their leader, his fat face red and freely perspiring, shot me a look, blue eyes squinted to questioning slits. "What did it look like?"

They never ask "when or where," but always, "What did it look like?" I had the answer: "Like a basketball without Wilson's name on it." I turned to point behind me to the middle of the fenced yard and blacktopped court where, despite the heat, a dozen prisoners scrambled happily after my nephew and the basketball he rose with into the air to slam through the hoop. "That's my nephew, John," I explained, consciously striving to keep the hurt from my voice. "That's him taking the ball out now. We're here because of flying saucers. The judge gave us six months but threatened us with five years apiece if we didn't plead guilty, and they kept any reference to the

14

UFO's out of the court records."

"Yeah, sure, man," the fat guy agreed, wiping the sweat with his hand from his face. "The government always covers it up. Like those guys in black. What did you see?"

"It's not just what we saw. I saw them a long time ago when I was a kid. We owned a farm. I'm the oldest of eight kids. Back when we saw the UFO's I was only thirteen. John's dad was a year younger. The night it happened our dad was away. I don't remember where, but with mom, there were nine of us at home. It was still mostly country around the farm then. No new houses or small farms the way it is today. No paved roads through the woods or public lighting on the road. When it got dark the trees and fields all melted together into an inky, velvet blackness. On a cloudy night you could barely see your hand in front of your face. It was like that. No moon or stars, just inky dark outside the windows.

"It was still early because the little kids weren't in bed yet. We were together in the front room, watching television, all except John's dad. He was out in the barn. He saw them first. They were across the fields above the trees about a half-mile away. I remember him running into the house, all excited, yelling for us to come see the flying saucers.

"I think we thought he was goofy, because we were laughing; I guess convinced he was joking, and the joke was on us for playing along with him, but the UFO's were still there: two bright orange balls, hovering together, low in the dark sky across the fields.

"They looked about the size of basketballs. Then one of them dropped below the horizon, or a line of trees and the horizon, and a moment later, the other had crossed the fields and stopped, a flat disc without any sides or top, floating directly above us.

"It didn't make a sound and was maybe a hundred feet up in the sky. It looked about fifteen feet across, and sort of whirled around inside itself like a windswept fire spins around inside a fifty-gallon drum, but there was no heat you could feel.

"We just stood there in the yard, staring up at it, not talking. Just watching it, it might have been watching us. I don't know how long we stood there like that. Then, it was just suddenly above the trees across the fields. The other one came up from behind it. They hung there for a minute, then just shot straight up into the sky, disappearing."

"What happened?"

"Nothing, then. That's all. We went back inside the house, filing in along behind Mom and one another. I was excited to have seen a UFO, and I could sense the others were too, but nobody said anything. Not a word. At least, not then, and as far as I know, not ever. Not to one another.

"That's the strangest part, and I sometimes wondered about it, but never seemed to remember to bring it up around Mom or the others. Anyway, being the eldest, I inherited the farm. Then when his dad died, John came to live with me and the wife. His dad was thirty-three when he died from some kind of rare form of blood disease. The doctors never did identify it. They didn't know what to do. He just sort of wasted away.

"It was John who told me of my brother's interest in UFO's. He'd told John that only people the UFO's were interested in ever saw them. That there was something special or important about such people, like maybe they were going to be President of the United States, or do something to improve the world. He said he knew this because he had been aboard a UFO. He told John that it was not only on earth these people might be important. He said there were lots of other worlds, and sometimes people who saw UFO's were important to these other worlds."

"How did they get there?"

"John's dad said the UFO's took'em. That's not all. He believed they were coming back for him and would cure him; that his disease was just a way of taking him without anyone ever knowing. He believed they would be back for him, even if they had to dig him up from the grave to get him."

"What a chump," a little guy in the middle of the group snorted with a laugh. "When you're dead, you're dead."

"Yeah," I said frowning, letting my eyes skip around the circle of incredulous faces. "It sounded nuts to me too. I should have probably let it go, but it worried me. I had seen the UFO's. Then you hear all the stories about people being abducted. They don't always remember. Something has to jog their memories. How long had we stood in the back yard, staring at that disc? Had we all been abducted? Maybe there was time missing? I didn't know, and I can almost remember being on board a ship, but like I was asleep. You know, when you are dreaming and you're trying to wake up but can't? It's like that. Besides, how come we had never talked about it? I had a lot of questions, but only one thing for certain. I had seen the UFO's. They weren't swamp gas or Venus rising or hot weather balloons. Something or someone had been flying them.

"It was not knowing that eventually got me. Even John let it go. He finished school and went off to college. Then, when he came back, since there weren't a lot of jobs, he continued to stay with me and the wife, and to work on the farm.

"Working together everyday we began to talk again about the UFO's. The more we talked about them and his dad, the more he told me what his dad had said, the more curious I became to know the truth. There was only one way to find out. You see, if his dad's body was gone we would have proof."

"You robbed your own brother's grave?"

"No, no. We had to find out. There was nothing else we could do."

"So you dug him up?"

"No. We never did dig him up. We went to the cemetery. That's true. We got there just after midnight, and that was our first mistake. The grounds were beautiful during the day with big oaks, the sun shining on a fishpond and huge spotted, red and yellow goldfish, the smell of the lawns fresh cut and bushes and manicured hedges, but at night, it was spooky, all shadows straight out of a horror movie. No lights. The trees blowing and lowing in the wind. It sounded like the dead moaning, but we had gone too far to back out; otherwise, we would have been gone from there.

"We knew right where the grave was and found it quick enough, but already spooked, to actually start digging it up was the hardest thing I ever did.

"This was my brother's grave. I knew it wasn't right to dig him up, and knew what John had to be feeling. We were more than a little convinced he wouldn't be there, but what if he was? After eight, almost ten years in the grave, what would we find? The way people are buried now they turn to goo, resembling a slimy mess like a huge, squeezed bar of wet soap. It wasn't the picture I wanted myself or John to have to live with for the rest of our lives."

"Did you do it?"

"We started digging, but by the time we had the dirt out of the hole and the shovel was scraping the vault, the groundskeeper or

19

watchman, I guess, had heard us and called the cops."

"You never found out?"

"Oh, yeah, we found out. You know the cops. They said they couldn't tell if we were shoveling dirt out or putting it back into the grave. A judge gave them a court order to open the vault and remove the casket a couple of days later."

"What did they find?"

"Nothing. He was gone."

"Com'on, man," the fat guy complained. "There had to be a body."

I shrugged. "That's what the cops thought too. They wanted us to give it back."

"They didn't believe you?"

"Do you?"

"You had proof."

"We knew the truth. All we had was what the cops had. A missing body. They couldn't believe us. It would have meant that everything they believed was wrong. In the end, they offered us a deal. We took it. No jury would have believed us."

"What about John? What's he believe?"

"That they came for his dad. That he's up there, out there on another planet somewhere. He expects him to come back someday."

"What was he like?"

"John's dad? You should talk to John. Read the book. It's all in there. What his dad said. What their many worlds without disease or poverty are like. There is a place for everyone. It tells us what we can do to bring him back. That's the good news. We have the choice. We aren't helpless. If we have faith and cooperate and help one another, he'll be back. It's our own destructive aggressiveness that keeps us from joining him. The reason he is important, he's the bridge between us and them."

"You believe that? You think he's coming back?"

"I can tell you what I know, but sometimes lately I find myself watching for him, looking up to the sky, knowing he is coming back." I pushed myself up, getting to my feet, standing, smiling sadly, and looking at their expectant faces. I felt sorry for them, and just as sorry for myself, knowing they could never know what I knew. "I knew him," I said, turning away. "I saw the UFO's. Talk to John. Read the book. You'll see. If we're ever going to join them, he's the way. When we are ready, he'll be back."

NO WAR STUFF ABOUT GOD, ANYMORE

Here's more truth than most people like to admit. On the other hand, it ain't that easy to ignore. Sometimes the answer to, "Where do they bury the survivors?" is, "they don't bury survivors."

No War Stuff About God, Anymore

The phone rang like the shot of a starter's pistol. Rich, shoving me, was off. Laughing, he leapt through the open kitchen door. I went after him, over and around chairs through the dining room. He bumped the big Christmas tree in the front room, taking no notice as it teetered to fall. Catching it meant I forfeited the race. The prickling branches, bouncing with lights and ornaments, were surprisingly heavy. Rich, hooting in triumph, snatched the receiver from the cradle of the phone on the end table beside the couch.

"Joe's Mortuary," he giggled. "You stab 'em we slab 'em."

Steadying the tree, the pine scent strong in the room, I stood looking at him. Earlier I'd said my old man was sick. I'd said he was dying. It was just something I said. Maybe wishful thinking. My old man was a mean drunk with fast hands. He liked using them and didn't have the right. He couldn't even hold a job. The night before, after spending the day at a labor service, he'd come home sober for once. He'd gone to bed early, telling Mom his ear ached and his head hurt. I'd hoped then he was dying, but I didn't like Rich clowning around about it.

He was a big oaf; fourteen, two years older than me, and nearly a head taller and at least thirty pounds heavier. We were in seventh grade

24

together at Saint Mary's and more or less friends. He was an only child and both parents worked, so there were no adults around to tell us what to do, which said a lot about him, and explained why he would answer the phone goofy like that and stand giggling in someone's ear.

I moved next to him. Words were buzzing out of the receiver like angry bees. Rich, straightening, listened with his mouth open and eyes wide.

"Yes, m'am, I will," he said. "Yes, m'am. Yes, m'am," he repeated. The receiver clicked. He rolled his eyes, looking at me, and just from that I had a bad feeling. "Your mom," he said, hanging up. "You gotta go home."

"Didn't she want to talk to me?"

"Nah. You better go. You coming back?"

"Yeah," I shrugged. "You know... if I can."

If I didn't go, Mom would ground me or put Rich's house off limits. I couldn't guess why she had phoned, wanting me home. She knew I hated my old man's drinking. If he was really sick and not hung over seeing pink elephants or whatever drunks saw, there wasn't anything I could do about it.

I picked my coat off the couch. It was heavy wool, designed with big black and white checks, the black nylon lining was quilted and warm enough. Good in the cold. I thought the wide collar cool, the way it turned up, like something Elvis would wear.

"Hey Mike," Rich said. "You know this one? Who buries the survivors?"

I finished buttoning up as Rich followed me into the front hall. "I don't know, man. Who buries the survivors?"

"They don't bury survivors."

"That ain't funny."

"Yes it is."

Opening the front door, I punched Rich hard in the chest. He tried returning it, but I was too quick for him, and was out the door, slamming it behind me. Laughing, I hurried across the wooden porch and down the snow covered stairs, into the cold. The punch made us even.

The air was full of tiny swirling flakes that fell and blew out of the sky. They clung to my coat and hair, melting against my face. The freezing winds gusted, pushing me along the icy sidewalk. Traffic was heavy, the tires splashing past in the slush covered street. Chicago always wet and dirty during winter, and I kind of liked the fallen snow when it was fresh and stuck and covered the city under a clean white blanket. Of course, it always melted, and I hated what was left, sodden and gray in the wind and cold. I snuggled down into my coat, pulling my collar up, glad I didn't have far to go: half a block up Diversey, the same down Lincoln.

Turning off Diversey onto Lincoln, I looked through the tall, steamy windows of a corner liquor store. Sometimes my old man hung around with the clerk. They were war buddies from Korea or something. I didn't really know, but it was a habit, looking for my old man in the liquor store. He wasn't there. His buddy was alone, sitting with a newspaper spread on the counter in front of him.

I didn't really think my old man was dying. He'd been a war hero and was still young and only thirty-three. He was tall, six feet, and thin, one-hundred forty pounds. And even with all his drinking, he was healthy. He was strong too. One time he'd taken his shirt off and had covered his solar plexus with his hand telling me to hit him in the stomach.

"Go ahead," he'd said. "Com'on. Hit me as hard as you can."

At first I'd been afraid, but he'd kept insisting.

"What are you, a chicken?" he'd teased. "You ain't afraid. Com'on, Mike. Don't be no chicken. Are you a chicken? Com'on, little chicken. Show me you're not chicken."

He'd made it so I'd had to do it. Then I'd wanted to do it. It hadn't mattered what he might do later. Right then he'd been sober. I couldn't very well be punished for obeying him. And he'd never hesitated to hit me. It had been my chance. Counting three real fast, I'd punched him as hard as I could, right in the stomach.

Geez, I'd felt it all the way up my arm, and all he'd done was smile. He hadn't said anything. He hadn't even looked at me. He'd gone over to sit on the couch. He'd picked up a throw pillow, pressing it against his stomach, still smiling, and his eyes on the television screen across the room.

Later Mom said I shouldn't have done it. She could always twist everything around. She'd blamed me. She'd said he was like a child and I was big for my age. I was wrong and old enough to know better. It hadn't mattered what he'd wanted or what he'd said. I shouldn't have listened to him. What if I had hurt him? What then? She hadn't tried to understand. I wasn't that big. I was the smallest kid in my homeroom at school. As far as I knew, nothing hurt him. Mom hadn't seen him smiling. He wasn't hurt, and besides, I was the kid, not him.

I wasn't smiling on Lincoln Avenue. I didn't remember ever being so cold. My face was frozen and felt about to fall off to shatter into a million pieces. By the time I had reached the hardware store with its sale bills plastering the windows, advertising half off spring gardening supplies, and had opened the door into the narrow hall and steep wooden stairs up to our apartment above the store, all I could think about was getting warm.

I went up the stairs two at a time in record time and crossed the landing to bust through the door. The oil heater sat in the dining room in the middle of the back wall, across from the front door. It was brown enameled metal about four feet high, three feet wide, and two deep, with a grating across the top. Unbuttoning my coat, I stood leaning into the rising heat. You could hear the fire burning inside the cabinet.

It was the only piece of furniture in the dining room. My old man had installed it. He'd stood on a high, rickety stepladder, sawing a hole for the stovepipe through the ceiling and then he'd gone into the attic, cutting a second hole through the roof, running the pipe outside. He'd seemed to know what he was doing and to enjoy doing it. He'd joked with Mom and had whistled under his breath while fitting the pipe sections together. I really didn't know what he liked, and didn't really care, so it didn't matter what he did. Most of the time he was too drunk to even hold a saw. Besides we had steam heat. It rattled up from the basement in old pipes to the iron radiators that stood in the corners of the rooms and sometimes leaked and dripped onto the hardwood floors. Mostly they worked okay, but Mom, who always said she was quoting my old man, said we couldn't depend on others. If you wanted anything done right, you had to do it yourself. She wouldn't depend on the landlord or coal trucks delivering coal to the basement on time. Not as long as she had three kids to worry about keeping warm, except it wasn't much of a worry. Although at times the radiators were icy cold to touch, and coming in from the cold to stand, thawing out in the rising heat, really felt good, we could have managed without the oil heater.

Too bad my old man didn't fix the lights. The rooms were huge and dark with gloomy half-light. The bulbs overhead in the ceiling fixtures were yellow and dingy, like dim candles, attaching deepening shadows to everything. The windows on either side of the apartment looked out on close brick walls. The only real light came in during the day through the bay windows in the front room. They were built over the street and you could stand in the bay, looking out and watching the traffic and people below on Lincoln Avenue.

The dining room was connected with the front room through a wide opening where narrow sliding partitions had been removed; the brass tracks were still visible in narrow slits cut across the floorboards and overhead across the ceiling. Liz and David were in the front room, sitting together on the floor, watching television. For a change, they were being quiet. They looked like little dolls in candle shop windows with big eyes and small, pale faces, blue with the screen's light. Yosemite Sam chased Bugs Bunny through a castle, blasting with his six-guns.

My parent's bedroom door opened on the dining room and was beside the front door. Mom came out, pulling the door closed behind her. She was wearing her flowered white housecoat and stopped and stood staring into the front room. Her long, black hair was disheveled and not brushed or pinned. She had that glazed, empty look on her face my old man sometimes had in his

30

eyes when he was looking through you at something far away.

Before marrying my old man, Mom had been a model. She'd given it up for him and had told me he'd looked so handsome and had been so certain of himself and confident in his uniform, she would have done anything for him. Then I had come along and later Liz and David. She said the war had changed my old man. That he'd had dreams it had taken away. Now Mom mostly had everything to do herself for my old man and for us. It was her life to worry about the rent and food and to beg free tuition for me at Saint Mary's, and for Liz and David, when they were old enough for school. She worked a lot of temporary jobs, mostly at night. She was working now, stuffing photos of kids on Santa's lap, so we would have a Christmas. She could have earned a lot of money, except my old man didn't want it. I couldn't figure him out. We needed the money and Mom had to work anyway, so why couldn't she model? Even if she was my Mom, I could see she was still pretty. She looked like the magazine pictures of women with big eyes and high cheekbones and red lips. My old man made life hard and she went along with him.

We weren't more than five or six feet apart and she didn't see me. Then she did. "There you are!" she yelled, almost stamping her foot. "Your father is sick!"

"Yeah," I said, shrugging. She could have said hello. "What do you want?"

"Don't you answer me back like that," she said. She took a breath, lifting her head, the hair in front falling down. She pushed it up, holding it back. "I may have to go to the hospital with your father. I think you should be here. You'll need to help out."

"Is he dying?"

"He's not dying," she said, her voice too loud. "He's not well," she said. "I want you here. It's only right. If anything happens, you should be here."

Aunt Marge, Mom's younger sister, came heavily down the hall into the dining room from the kitchen. She was a big woman, but not only big, fat, but almost six feet tall. She wasn't much like Mom. Marge worried about her size and always told people she was dieting, and never did. She did wash a lot and scrubbed herself until I saw her skin reddened and raw. She smelled of soap and body lotions and of something unique and not unpleasant, but I couldn't guess. She stopped in the hall entrance and stood looking at me while nibbling a graham cracker. She had big black eyes and nibbled with her front teeth, like a scared little mouse. The incongruity struck me funny. She was a dainty elephant. I smiled at her, and she was always okay by me. I was glad to see her.

"Marge can baby-sit," I said. "I don't have to stay here."

"This is your home," Mom said. "Your father is sick. Don't you understand?"

She looked at Marge, appealing for support. There was something more in the look that passed between them. Something I saw and didn't understand.

"Please," Mom said when Marge remained silent. "You should want to be here. You'll wish someday you had been. He's your father."

"Try to understand," Marge said.

"He's not sick!" I yelled, feeling hot and trapped. "He's drunk again!"

"He's not drunk!" Mom shouted back, stamping her foot. Her face reddened. She moved towards me and stopped. "Don't you say that again. Don't you ever say that about your father. He's right about you. You've got a smart mouth. No one can tell you anything. You're not to leave this house!"

She quickly turned and went to the bedroom door, opening it and disappearing inside, the door closing behind her. She would probably tell him what I'd said. I didn't care. She wasn't honest. I hadn't been smart mouthed, telling the truth. He was a drunk, denying it didn't change anything or make it go away. We all had problems because of him. If she didn't remember, I did. One time he'd hit her. I'd secretly called the police. They had arrested him at the liquor store and he'd spent the night in jail for being drunk, and would have stayed there, except she'd lied to them, saying he hadn't hit her. And once he'd come home so drunk he couldn't make it to the

33

apartment door and had slept in the stairwell, a whiskey bottle cradled in his arms like a baby. It had been embarrassing to see him like that when I'd opened the front door and found him. I had almost wanted to cry. That was what drunks did and what he did, embarrassing us. Not caring about our feelings or about anything or anyone, except himself and where his next drink was coming from.

"You should love your father," Marge said. She had moved over close beside me. "No matter what you think now, Mikey. He's still your father. You should love him."

I could almost forgive Marge. She didn't have to live with him and didn't know. He called her on the phone, telling her he needed a babysitter and she came. He bought her silver kisses, little chocolate teardrops, and gave her money for coming and afterwards walked her home through the dark streets to her empty rooms. She appreciated his concern and thought him considerate, and like everyone else, she admired him for being a war hero, but with her there was more to it. She once told me he was too sensitive for what the war demanded of him. From the way she said it, kind of in awe and whispering, and maybe seeing what she was saying, just the way she looked; I had stared at her, wondering if she wasn't in love with him. I'd though she was. She certainly was good at defending him, and now, standing beside me in the dining room, she was doing it again.

"Give him a chance," she told me, putting her hand on my arm. "He has been through so much you'll never understand."

I didn't need her making excuses for him, and I didn't have to listen to her. I pulled away from her and went to the front room, crossing to stand at the windows. I didn't look back or hear her leave the dining room.

The heat in the apartment had fogged into moisture on the windows. Wiping it from the cold panes with my hand, I wiped my wet hand dry on my pants. It was still snowing. There weren't any people walking. The passing cars moved steadily, splashing through a deepening river of slush. It was odd how the weather could match your feelings. Like when you were cold inside and it was cold outside or when someone died and was buried and it rained. The sky seemed to cry for them. But there was nothing to it. The dead were buried when they died, rain or shine, and you could feel stormy and angry inside without a cloud in the sky.

Sometimes my old man would quit drinking for days and even weeks. It never mattered. It didn't last. He said himself he liked the taste of liquor. When he would quit, it was a matter of time until he went back to it. Besides, he was more crazy sober. Mostly he was sort of distracted, but had this way of giving a sudden start. Then you knew he was gone inside his head. Sometimes, drunk or sober, though mainly sober, he would suddenly stop in the street and stand stock still, rising up on his toes as he turned around and just stared back down the street, his eyes wide and searching where he'd just been, like he'd missed something important or was expecting something or someone to pop out of the ground and he had to be ready. Everyone knew what he was doing —looking for the enemy. It was embarrassing. I didn't care what he had been through, even if it was an awful lot and was terrible. Others had done it and gotten over it. He could have, except he kept living it, holding onto the memory, until there was only the past and no future. He had made himself crazy.

I hadn't believed he'd hurt me. At least not the way he'd hurt people in the war. Sometimes he scared me with his look like a hawk about to pounce on a mouse. Then I would avoid him, just in case he forgot who I was. Only, mostly, he wasn't sober, and drunk he was mean and, in some ways, less crazy. He brooded when drinking, occupied with himself. He knew where he was and what he'd done, and if his mood could go from bad to worse in a split second, you knew he was seeing you, so that he seemed less dangerous, except for his quick hands.

I was proud to think he'd been a hero; there wasn't much good to remember about him. When I was six-years old he'd come home on leave. Almost the whole time he and Mom were gone, leaving me with Marge. Then one day he'd borrowed a car. He'd taken us out of the city to Fox Lake, north of Chicago, for a picnic in the forest preserves along the lake, and even that went wrong.

I'd had a dog then, Pepper. A small black terrier. No problem to anyone. I'd loved Pepper and he'd loved getting out in the grass and trees and running on the beach. Mom had laughed a lot while Pepper and I played on the sand. My old man had swum way out in the water until his head was a black dot, bobbing in the distance. When he'd swum back, he'd grilled steaks and hotdogs. We had eaten all day and had all we wanted. Not all we wanted, but all we could eat. It was swell like that with us all together, and would have been the best time, but Pepper was gun-shy. When my old man started the car to leave, it backfired and Pepper ran away.

We had searched for him, driving through the trees around the lake. I was already in tears when my old man had said we had wasted enough time. He'd also said Pepper was a dog and could take care of himself. Mom said my old man had done everything he could, but it wasn't true. We had left when we could have kept looking.

Afterwards, he'd returned to the Army. He'd come home just long enough to take Pepper away and to get Mom on his side. I'd cried a lot after that, thinking; if I was lost, would they abandon me?

Two years later I was eight-years old and my old man came home to stay. It was the same thing. Mom and he together with him drinking and teasing and slapping me across the back of my head to make certain he had my attention. And Mom pregnant with Liz and then David, defending my old man. She would always say he was my father. She meant he was her husband. She loved him and putting him up there with God. He could do no wrong and for her there was no one else. So now if he was sick and Mom might lose him, I didn't know if I could really care what happened.

I heard Mom open the bedroom door. She closed it and went down the hall to the kitchen. I had to listen hard through the cartoon noises to hear as she told Marge that she didn't care what my old man had said, they had to call a doctor. Marge mumbled something. Then Mom shouted, pleading, "Don't start that! Don't cry! Please!"

I didn't hear the rest. I didn't know if Marge was crying, maybe Mom too. It seemed to me they should have already called a doctor. Mom knew my old man would be against it. It was the way men were, and he was good at that. He wouldn't call a doctor, even if he knew he needed one.

He couldn't support us and was running away, hiding in a bottle, but he knew what a man was supposed to do. Some nights he would come into my bedroom. He'd wake me up while he sat on the floor, his back against the wall, the orange glow of his cigarette dancing in the dark, the smoke and smell of his boozy breath filling the air, drunk, as he talked about being a man.

His stories and words frightened me. He would always say there was something he wanted me to know. Something I knew I didn't want to know, and knew he was going to tell me anyway. I couldn't get away from him. He'd told me he'd had to put his thumbs through a man's throat. He'd said it was war and there and never been a good war, and wars were always a crime, but you had to go, even if you knew it was wrong, because it was your duty. Besides, they would shoot you if you didn't go. He'd also told me there was no God. It hadn't shocked me. I wasn't even surprised. For a long time I had suspected God was like Santa Claus and heaven as empty as the North Pole.

So, I'd been listening, and at breakfast I'd asked Mom. She had sighed and sat down at the table, blinking and staring at me. Of course there was a God. We just had to believe. Later, I'd heard her tell my old man not to tell me 'war stuff about God anymore.'

He must have thought I'd betrayed him by running to Mom. He wouldn't speak to me, or even look at me. For a long time he didn't come to my room. I had hoped he'd forgotten me, but he hadn't.

His voice woke me. He'd pulled the lowboy dresser out from the wall and over in front of the open bedroom door. He was sitting cross-legged, Indian style on top of the dresser. The hall ceiling light behind him had made him a black shadow, except for a glow around his head, like the halos of plaster saints. He was smoking, the gray cloud lazily floating around him.

"... no God," he'd said. "I love your mother. That's all right, Mike. It's a good thing. But she doesn't know. You think I don't know? I know, Mike. Wouldn't I change it, if it could be changed? I want you to know. We could all go to heaven. It ain't like that. At school. The sisters and the priests. It's not just your mother. It's another way of being crazy. You see that? Don't let them bet your life. They'll try. You can't get it back. Next time someone dies, we'll go see them. I'll take you myself. Me and you, Mike. You touch them. I want you to touch them. They're gone. What's left isn't anything. It wouldn't matter if we threw it in the street."

He'd lowered his head, holding the cigarette in his mouth. I could smell the liquor across the room where I laid in bed, the blanket pulled up tight to my chin. I hadn't dared to breathe, hoping he had passed out or was asleep. Then he'd lifted his head, laughing to himself.

"You go to heaven because they shoot the hell out of you," he'd said, continuing to laugh. "That's funny, a joke, Son. You think I'm crazy? I've seen them die. I've laid with them in their blood. It's quick. I knew them. You don't just die. They're friends. It's messy, Mike. They call for God. They're crying. You think men don't cry? We all do it. You're dying. You're scared. And there ain't no good reason. Don't let them do it to you. You touch them. When they're dead. I want you to touch them. You have to know. It's all gone."

I remembered that part and there was more before he'd left, leaving the dresser across the door, as if he meant to return. I'd covered my head, hiding under the blanket, thinking he might come back and how there was no God, and how horrible, and how it took a long time to die with lots of blood. So I knew what it meant to be a man and know these things, and I wanted him to take it all back because it was his entire fault for telling me and it wasn't fair. I was just a kid.

Mom came out of the kitchen into the hall and through the dining room and across the front room to find me at the window staring out at the snow and traffic. "I'm going to the hospital with your father," she said. "I've called an ambulance. You do me a favor, Mikey. Let me know when it comes." She brushed her tears away with one hand and glanced uncertainly at Liz and David on the floor in front of the television. She looked at me, her eyes filling with tears. She tried to smile. "I'm depending on you, Mikey. You come tell me."

She went back across the front room and through the dining room to her bedroom door. I wondered what was going on inside the room and followed her, but stopped when she opened the door and I could see past her into the bedroom. The light was off, but I saw my old man lying on the far side of the bed, his face against the wall. He was naked, a long, ghastly pale shadow. A sheet was twisted around one foot. The other sheet and blankets were on the floor with the pillows. He moaned and rolled over onto his back and on over to his side, pulling his legs up against his chest. His hands covered his face. I felt kind of confused and nervous inside, like I might be sick. I hadn't ever seen him naked. It surprised me how he looked so exposed and helpless. For the first time I realized he might actually, really, die. I suddenly know what Mom meant about him being my father and was instantly sorry for him and maybe for myself. I wished things could have been different between us and that I'd never called the police on him that one time and hadn't hit him in the stomach. Mom shut the door. I was glad for not having to see him, but knew he was there. My heart beat faster than ever. I wanted him to forgive me. I felt hot all over. My coat was suddenly too heavy, smothering me. I pulled it off, slinging it down on the couch.

I hadn't noticed Marge standing in the dining room. Tears streaked down her round cheeks. She had a tissue and dabbed at her eyes with it, her shoulders continuing to shake. She was so big and so sad. She must have seen into the bedroom. Watching Marge, I knew if my old man died, Mom would need me. Marge wouldn't be any help. I didn't know how to comfort Marge and went back to the window, waiting for the ambulance.

I didn't cry. It wouldn't have been right. I couldn't reconcile how I felt about him actually dying. I thought how he was my father and was a hero. I wanted to feel good about him and feel sorry for him. I hadn't forgotten what he'd done, embarrassing us, and destroying any reason for admiring him, but it didn't matter. I couldn't even blame him for dying. He had no control over it, but I had resented him and wished him dead, and now felt miserable with the memories of it. I knew if there had ever been a chance for his forgiveness, it waited in the future that would die with him. And then I was crying, silently, the unbidden tears filling my eyes and blurring the falling snow outside the window into a fuzzy grayness. But I had no right to cry, and angrily rubbed my eyes until I could see again.

Marge came and stood behind me. She continued to cry, her breath catching in her throat. I could feel her sighs, hot and kind of tickling on my neck. I was glad she was there. We didn't wait long. The squad car slid through the slush and traffic, its lights flashing blue in the snow as it entered the intersection, crossing Diversey. A white and orange striped ambulance was behind it. They stopped in the far lane across the street and waited for traffic to stop, then made a wide U-turn in front of the waiting cars and pulled up against the curb downstairs.

The ambulance was almost directly below our window. Two attendants in dark blue windbreakers and white pants climbed out of the cab. The taller one stopped and stood on the curb, slapping his arms against the cold while waiting for the two policemen to walk back from their car and join him. The other attendant came around the street and opened the ambulance's rear doors. He reached inside and pulled one end of a sheet covered stretcher and stood with it braced on his knee. The attendant with the police walked back, talking to them as he took the other end of the stretcher from the ambulance.

Marge touched my arm. "You go down and let them in," she said. "I'll tell Beth."

We crossed the room together. Liz and David know something was happening. They had turned up the television. The apartment seemed noisy and suddenly busy. Opening the apartment door I started down the stairs. I must have left the street door unlocked, because the policemen had let themselves into the building. They were big men dressed in blue uniform overcoats and gloves and their feet were heavy, tromping up the stairs single file in front of the ambulance attendants.

I was eager to help. "It's up here," I said, going down the stairs to meet them. "Come on up. I'll show you."

"What gives here, kid?" the leading policeman asked. He had a fleshy, red face under his hat. "Who's hurt? What's going on?"

"It's my old man," I told him, turning to lead the way back up to the apartment. "He's dying. Come on with me." It felt important to be helping them. "You can see for yourselves."

"Dying?" He sounded surprised, his voice, puzzled. "Your old man, huh?"

"Yeah," I yelled over my shoulder as I reached the landing. "We think he's dying."

Marge was standing in the open bedroom door, her back to me. The light was on. Mom stood at the foot of the bed. She had on her black long coat. My old man was still naked, lying with his face against the far wall. He must have somehow hurt himself. There was blood smeared on the wall and in his hair and on his shoulders and back. In the light his skin was yellow, the color of old newspapers. I knew he wasn't himself and wouldn't keep a blanket on or Mom would have covered him. She picked up the bed covers, folding and stacking them together with the pillows on the dresser behind her. She'd brushed her hair and had on lipstick. She looked tired and was pale with her eyes empty, staring at my old man.

Marge turned as the policemen entered the dining room. Her face was blotchy and eyes were red from crying. They nodded at her and moved back, out of the way, as the attendants rolled the stretcher through the door. I wondered if it would fit into the bedroom, but it fit okay, long ways, next to the bed. Mom came around behind the attendants to stop in the doorway, looking back into the bedroom. I went over and stood beside her. Marge stood behind me and the policemen were behind her across the room in front of the oil heater. The attendants folded down the stretcher and lifted it onto the mattress beside my old man. The short attendant was at the foot of the bed and stood leaning over the footboard, ready to lift my old man's legs when the other guy was ready. The taller man was kneeling on the mattress to reach over the stretcher. They did all this without speaking and seemed to know what they were doing. When they were ready and touched my old man, he swung his arms and legs, twisting free of their hands. He was really out of it and didn't know what was happening. They tried again, but again, couldn't hold him.

"Please," Mom begged. "Can't you help him?"

"Look, lady," the short attendant said, "That's what we're doing here." He was a rough guy and walked over in front of us, so that we had to step back out the door as he waved, signaling the policemen. "You guys want to get in here and give us a hand?"

The policemen didn't look happy. Exchanging frowns, the creases in their faces deepened as they slowly came over and entered the bedroom. Mom moved back into the doorway with me following her. The short attendant walked around the bed and pulled it away from the wall and went into the space he'd made. A policeman joined him, so that an attendant and policeman was then on either side of the bed with the stretcher on the mattress beside my old man. He wasn't moving, but his eyes had rolled back in their sockets with only the bloodshot whites showing. The men reached for him and he fought their hands, throwing himself into the air as he swung his arms and legs. They released what ever hold they had managed to grab and nodded and frowned, grunting but obviously didn't know what to do. They made another half-hearted attempt and he rolled against the stretcher and quickly jerked away, throwing himself back, his head striking the wooden headboard, loudly knocking it against the wall. He sat up with his eyes closed and mouth hanging open. His teeth were black. A reddening drool ran down his chin, dripping on his bare chest and stomach as he fell back onto the mattress. I looked up at Mom, wondering what she thought. She had her hand over her mouth with her eyes closed. Her heart was breaking. She'd married my old man for better or worse, loving and suffering with him, and mostly, from the beginning, only had a little of the one and a whole lot of the other. Now she was losing even that when he was her life and all she wanted. I didn't let myself remember she'd let us all suffer for his sake. Maybe she'd thought it was our duty to my old man, the same as she'd believed it was her duty, or maybe she hadn't known how to love her kids without feeling disloyal to him.

My eyes filled with tears. I didn't want to see anymore and turned away. Then Marge had her arms around me, holding me against her breasts. She was so soft and smelled so good, her hand in my hair, and her face streaked with tears, I couldn't help sobbing.

"Ooooh, God! I'll do anything! I'll believe in you! I promise. Ooooh God! I will! I promise! I'll be good! I will! I will!"

"Baby," Marge hushed me, the way she had when I was little and she'd held me, rocking me against her. "Shhh, baby. Shhh."

I was quieted and heard the men straining in the bedroom, but didn't look, and didn't know how they put him on the stretcher. When Marge released me she had to step back and Mom was moving back out of the way to let the policemen through the door into the dining room. I saw my old man on the stretcher. They had buckled cloth straps across him. He wasn't moving, except for his skin tightening against the ribs, rising with his chest heaving under the straps. They folded down the stretcher's wheels and covered his nakedness with an olive drab blanket they had brought with them that was stamped U.S. ARMY. I was still crying and was sorry for my old man and for us all, knowing this was how it ended.

Mom was behind the stretcher as the attendants
carried my old man down the stairs. The
policemen followed her down. I knew my old man
wouldn't be coming back and ran to the window.
Wiping my eyes, I shoved my face against the
glass and was numb to it being cold and wet.
Below in the snow that fell now fast and heavy in
great, huge flakes, darkening the sky, the
policemen went to their car and got in while the
attendants opened the ambulance and slid my old
man inside. The tall attendant helped Mom in and
climbed in with her. The short man swung the
doors shut behind them and went around in the
street to the cab. The ambulance started, the
orange siren lights spinning, flashing, as it
followed the squad car into traffic to disappear in
the snow that filled the air and was like a gray
curtain, closing behind them.

THE GEESE

If I told anyone this as the truth they would not believe. So here is the lie they will believe and say, "This is true." And it is. I joined the army to get away from the geese.

The Geese

The Geese

One year in the fall in the valley below the Sutter place, Milk River flooded the fields around Wolf Creek and the geese, in their migration south, flew out of Canada by the thousands to stop and feed on the wild grains. In the mornings, some of the geese were always trapped with their feet caught in the ice that formed around them where they had settled. Mr. Sutter kept the children home from school and sent four of the boys, ages eight, nine, ten, and thirteen down to the fields before sunrise in the cold and dark with hundred pound potato sacks and axes and hatchets to club the geese and hack off their feet frozen in the ice. The geese in their panic at being attacked made a lot of noise when clubbed and flopped around on the ice; when escaping, they rose, honking and flapping their wings in great, thundering white clouds, flying away.

The boys were flushed and excited, splashing the geese, and afterwards in the gray lit dawn, it was like picking berries, gathering the dead birds, except the bodies were wet and heavy and it was hard work, the boys beginning to shiver in the cold, knee deep, grassy waters while thinking about carrying the bulky sacks back across the valley to drag them home up the mountain.

The sun rose in the cloudless sky and the older girls came happily running down the rocky footpath in the warming air, their faces red and braided hair flying, laughing, pleased to meet the exhausted boys so nearly home, and glad to drag the heavy sacks the rest of the way up the trail. There was a general excitement in the yard that greeted them when they all arrived, like an unexpected holiday, with having the birds and cleaning them, the whole family in the yard, everyone working, dipping the geese in the boiling water of a fifty-gallon drum to pluck the steaming, feathered carcasses.

Feathers stuck wet to clothes and in hair and to faces and went everywhere, clinging to the playing children and grandchildren. Drying feathers floated, riding the light breeze, curling up into the sky and falling down lighter than snow, covering the scabrous yard of rocks and patchy weeds to be swept and swirled up and around and carried away by the wind for days afterwards.

The meat filled the freezer in the kitchen hall and the rusty freezer on the back porch outside the door. Mr. Sutter hung and smoked the remaining birds in the rickety shack between the house and hay barn and the meat lasted all winter, but winters came early on the mountain and were always long and cold and harsh, and there were plenty of winters in those years without any meat.

It helped that the government gave the Sutter girls with children and no husband's food stamps and powered eggs and condensed milk and blocks of cheddar cheese and dried beans and gallon cans of peanut butter. The girls sometimes worked in the potato fields and garden behind the house with Mrs. Sutter, planting small, red potatoes that grew in the stony soil and beans and corn and other things in the garden that would keep and could be dried or pickled and put up by them until needed. No one starved on potatoes and beans, but there were always more babies and growing grandchildren of varying shapes and sizes and differing hues.

Mr. Sutter thought the girls could do no wrong, but he was determined to make men out of the boys. As soon as they could lift an ax or swing a sickle he worked them like mules, sweating them from sunrise to sunset in the woods or haying fields, beating them regularly with whatever was at hand for any supposed infraction, breaking their spirits and reshaping them, domesticating, and hardening them for the world.

The boys wanted only to get away from home and one by one they left the mountain for jobs in Shelby or further south in the copper mines in Great Falls. The girls, even when old enough to leave, stayed on the mountain or else left it with some passing boy or man or some other vague infatuation or fancy only to soon return, most often with a baby in arms or in waiting..

Mr. Sutter converted the haying barn across the yard into a small house for the girls with bedrooms downstairs and the open loft into a dormitory upstairs. The girls painted it bright red with white trim and were happy to have their own house, although from time to time one or another of them would disappear, walking down the dirt road to the state highway and hitchhiking to

Shelby, declaring on her return, days or weeks or months later that she had been to town to see her brothers. Sometime one or another of the boys would drive up the mountain and stop in the yard with a missing sister in the car, bringing her home, and sometimes when one of the boys was married and started having children of his own he would visit to show Mrs. Sutter his family.

On these occasions Mr. Sutter always acted glad to see them, smiling at them from ear to ear when they pulled into the yard, but the welcome never lasted long and the visits always ended in arguments with the old man quoting from the Bible and telling them they were an ungrateful bunch of this and that after all he had done to make men of them.

The summer the youngest boy turned sixteen and was the only one left at home of any size, Mr. Sutter was already half crippled from limping on a bad hip joint. He was too old himself for hard work or to be of any real help and he hired an extra hand from off the Blackfoot Reservation to help with the haying and wood cutting, paying him room and board and a little extra with the food stamps the girls gave to Mrs. Sutter.

The hired man, Louis Kote, slept on a canvas cot in the smoke shack. He was a good worker and was tall and dark with black hair down his back and black eyes and perfect white teeth. His brown, bare, broad shoulders and deep chest, and long hard muscles were attractive to the girls. To them he seemed knowing and experienced, smiling at them with his eyes as fixed and as bright as a cat's, sizing up a mouse. In fact, for all his apparent confidence and easy ways, Louis was barely more than a boy alone in the world for the first time in his life. It was just his boy's dumb luck, which the young have for better or for worse that the job came with a house full of girls.

The girls pestered him constantly, visiting him at night in the shack, giving him little and almost no rest from his hard days labors. It did not take Mr. Sutter long to know what was up. In a sudden rage he attacked Louis, who, not wanting to hurt the old man, simply sidestepped his charge. Too slow to follow, Mr. Sutter tripped over his own tangling feet and sprawled on his belly in the yard in the weeds and dirt in front of the girls and grandchildren and in front of his old woman and youngest son who had hurriedly followed the old woman out of the house to the porch to see what the old man was shouting about.

The brothers who had left, on hearing about the old man's fall, thought it a good story to tell on him, and then, when Louis came down to Shelby and joined the Army, telling the recruiter he was enlisting to get away from the women, the brothers all laughed until tears streamed from their eyes and their sides hurt and they could not laugh anymore from fear of wetting their pants.

Mrs. Sutter was the first to die. She had never been more than ten miles from the mountain, as she had been born across the valley at Tree Forks and at fourteen years old had been given in marriage to the twenty-seven year old Tom Sutter. She left behind eleven girls and six boys and thirty-three grandchildren. Her passing seemed to change everything. Some of the girls and their children moved over to the main house, and before long, old man Sutter began selling off most of the eight hundred acres he had bought with the money the boys had earned in the woods and haying fields over the years. Huge, expensive houses were built across the valley on the hills there to overlook the meandering river. The county built new roads and paved old dirt roads, including the dirt road up the mountain and past the Sutter place. The grandchildren grew up fast and some of the older Sutter girls and their daughters found new husbands, or first time husbands, and the male grandchildren brought wives to the mountain. New and used house trailers were hauled up the paved road to squat in their own small, rocky lots. Pickups and cars were parked helter-skelter and abandoned along the road and in fields and in front of and beside and behind trailers and even in the Sutter yard. Someone always seemed to be having a baby. People, having long memories, started calling the mountain "Indian Hill." The name stuck, although the old man seemed not to hear it.

The brothers watched the land sold and the money spent to support the girls and their families, and with all the changes on the mountain, they knew it would all be gone soon. They said the old man was not taking it with him.

Mr. Sutter did not get around much, but every year in the fall, he stood in the yard among the rusting cars and trucks, watching the sky for the geese to fly over the mountains in their V-formations like bombers. Sometimes you could

almost hear him wishing to himself that the river
would flood its graveled banks and he could again
send his boys into the fields for the geese he knew
would stop and be frozen in the mornings with
their feet caught in the ice. The year he died the
fields around Wolf Creek did flood and the geese
flew down in their migration south, but the water
did not ice and the birds in their huge flocks flew
away unmolested. The girls sold what little was left
to them by the old man and moved to Shelby and
further south, some as far away as California; the
houses and shack torn down and replaced by
house trailers.

IN THE CLEARING STANDS

Courage is never enough.

In the Clearing Stands

In the Clearing Stands

When I opened the door Pioa was
reading, stretched out on his rack in skivvies, his
brown face shadowed by the evening twilight
grays filtering through the tinted window pane in
the back wall above our bunks. Our beds were
side by side under the window with a small table
between them. We each had a metal wardrobe
against the walls at our bunk's foot, and there was
a desk with a lamp just to the right of the door.

With the door open, the hall light spilling
into the room, I crossed to my wardrobe and
opened the flimsy shutters on a formation of
khakis. The creased sleeves hung sharp, in a
regulation row, decorated with Special Services
insignia and three yellow-gold buck sergeant's
chevrons.

Pioa's bunk springs squeaked in
complaint as he turned to roll on his side towards
me. "You coming or going?" he asked.

"Both," I said, reaching up to the
crowded shelf for the blue canvas fight bag,
containing my ring gear. I jerked the bag's
shoulder strap, careful to pull it out, away from
my neatly hung uniforms.

"What's up?" he asked

"I've got a fight." I did not like springing it on him like this. We were buddies, pals. I knew how he would feel, being left out again. Only this time he would be on his own, knowing I had finally been scheduled to fight. There was no easier way than to just say it: "I'm going now."

He sat up. "Tonight? You're on the card tonight? How did this happen?"

"I just heard." Despite his shaved heard and a pock marked faced, he looked and sounded younger than twenty-two; more like some anxious kid, waiting for a bed time story before being tucked in for the night. There was nothing I could do to help him, and it did not help my feelings any that the night outside, melding with the hall light reflecting off the glass, had turned the window into a dark mirror. My silhouetted image from the waist up stared back at me, a weird cardboard puppet in a shadow play. "Hagie was downstairs when I came out of the rec-room. The Coach sent him to find me. They need a heavy weight. I'm elected."

"Terry didn't tell you?"

"No. I just heard."

"Who you fighting?"

"I don't know."

"You don't know?"

"Hagie didn't know."

"He knew" he said, stubbornly. "He just didn't tell you. When's the last time you fought? You better watch out, Jack. Maybe you get what Indians always get."

"They only know I'm Indian because I told them. Anyway, don't you mean Native American?"

Generally, Pioa would have been correcting me, since I believed anyone born in America was Native American and thought of us as Indians. Although I was dark I did not look Indian, with my black eyes and wavy black hair. My Dad was Blackfoot with my Mom being Irish. Nor was I very Indian acting, and probably would not have survived long on a reservation, but I was skin enough to understand Pioa's grievances and usually stood with him, offering him my support, but not now.

"Maybe you'd like me to turn down the fight and hang around here, bitching about it? "I made a demon face, eyes bulging, and tongue hanging out. "We were robbed!"

"Who said that?"

"Some fighter. Maybe the same guy who said, "I should have stayed in bed."

"It ain't that. "

"Good because I'd hate to think you've given up."

"I know."

"Yeah. But you still want me to quit. Off with their heads, right? You want a war whoop? Anyway, I ain't heard no owl screeching lately."

"I heard it."

"Me," I said. "You ain't me. I make my own way. Don't try to save me. I'll save myself. Did you think the Captain could keep us out of the ring forever?"

"It's too late for the Olympic Trials."

"Maybe not. After I win tonight, you don't know. Maybe it will be different."

"I though we were friends, Jack."

"We are, but we aren't attached at the hip." I meant it to be funny. His eyes widened, than narrowed. "You take everything too serious," I said, looking around to see my hooded sweatshirt, hanging in the shadows behind the door. I retrieved it and pulled it over my head. "I'll need this on the way back," I said, turning around to face him. "Look, I don't like this any better than you do. I didn't tell you but I went to the recruiters. If I re-up they'll transfer me. Maybe I'll go to Germany. I've got it figured out. Another seventeen years and I can retire. But I can't transfer unless Captain Brooks releases me. Otherwise, I'm stuck here for the duration of my enlistment. Anyway, I ain't sure about staying in. I've got to fight. If I win maybe I'll stick around.

If not, then I'll be out in six months. I've been thinking about going home."

"I thought we were in this together."

"We are, man, except that was before I made up my mind to quit. If we were boycotting because they wouldn't let us fight, I'm fighting. Either way, I've got to do what's best for me."

"If you fight, maybe the Captain won't release you. Send Hagie back to the gym without you. It won't make any difference. We'll take a cab ride to town to see Nina."

"I already sent Hagie. To tell Coach and Terry I'll be there. I'm gonna jog across base to warm up for the fight. Why don't you come and go with me?"

"They don't want me," he said, lying back down on his side. "I'll come to the hospital to see you later."

"Don't bury me yet," I said, adjusting the bag's strap to slip it over my shoulder. The bag hung down against my hip, so that I hardly noticed it. "Don't worry. They'll let you fight soon."

"You don't know."

"Maybe after I win tonight."

"Sure. Good luck."

"I wish you'd go with me. You want me to switch on the lamp?"

He shook his head. "You know what book this is?" He asked. "Heart of Darkness."

"I'll take my chances."

"In the hospital?"

"No. You seen the nurses? Four eyes. They look like owls."

There was no more to say. Pulling the door closed behind me, left him laying alone in the dark. I shook the image from my head as I went downstairs, through the glassed entrance into the night. The breeze was cool and gritty with sand, so that I pulled up the sweatshirt hood as I trotted along the narrow sidewalk and out into the empty street, jogging under the orange glare of the overhead sodium-neon lights.

The quickest way across the fort was in a straight line which also happened to be the shortest way; three blocks of withered and treeless lawns of red brick barracks which resembled saltine boxes on their sides with rows of yellow windows stacked three stories high beneath a vaporous mauve sky gradually darkening above the flat roofs. Then, through the A.I.T. training complex to the parade grounds, across the parade grounds to another block of saltine boxes, then through the maze of the ruins of the old fort to the main drag and post commissary, and around behind the commissary to cross the road into the gym's parking lot under the rows of spotlights

63

along the domed roof. A little more than two miles, and I felt good, the night shadows and flat hush familiar and my legs strong, working only enough to start a sweat.

The lawn's rotating water jets came on, erupting into splashing arches, their sputtering slaps mingling with the rhythm of my echoing boots. The sun scorched grasses flooded and obsidian rivulets flowed along the curbs to stream into the gutters. A breeze rose cold and dry, tainted by the fetid scents carried across the desert from the distant foot hills, the wind sweeping it in over the plateau of ashy sand dunes to mix with the isolated fort's brunt breath of concrete and tar.

Along the curb ahead a gray and black lettered tin sign hung chained between two white metal posts, announcing:

ADVANCED INFANTRY TRAINING
C COMPANY
10TH BATTALION-THIRD DIVISION

I swung left pass the sign to cross a wet lawn onto a narrow sidewalk, following it through a maze of identical two-story brick barracks. Shaved-tail trainees in white t-shirts moved silently behind the wide barracks' windows of dormitories cluttered with rows of stacked bunks and metal lockers under bright florescent ceiling lights. They were confined at night for the length of their training, the same as I had been almost three years earlier, when the possibilities of army life were new and strange.

I had finished basic with the distinction of being the only trainee chosen from a company of 300 men to be sent to NCO Training school at Fort Polk, Louisiana. After taking A.I.T. at Fort Polk, I transferred to Airborne Basic at Fort Benning, Georgia. From there I was assigned to an 82nd Airborne Division at Fort Bragg. I had proven myself in the training, and now more then anything I missed it, and regretted the fact I had missed Desert Storm. The transfer to Special Services was my own fault. I volunteered for the boxing squad at Bragg. This was boxing with head gear and a point system with two minute rounds restricted to three rounds. It was fun. Supposed to be fun. Shake hands and no hard feelings afterwards. It was possible to get seriously hurt, or to hurt someone, but mostly the referees looked out for the fighters and stopped the bouts if necessary. I won six matches in a row. Unfortunately, fate must have decided to take a hand. I got 'lucky', knocking out the last opponent in the third round of the sixth fight with a full bird colonel from Special Services present at ringside. He was impressed enough to order captain Brooks from Fort Bell to interview me about joining the Special Services Boxing Program, including training, and perhaps qualifying for the Olympics. What I did not know until later was that boxing at Bell was serous business with all the fun squeezed out of it

At Bragg the Company Commander sent for me. When I arrived he left me alone in his office with the obese Captain Brooks. He sat behind the desk, his hat still on his head. His blue, red-veined eyes bulged in his flat face with its wide nose and thick fleshy lips that held a long, smoking green cigar that filled the room with a sweet herbal smell. He gave me the look a frog squatted down to eye a circling fly would.

I came to attention in front of the desk, saluting as I reported, "Sir, Corporal Autry, as ordered, sir."

He gestured indifferently without returning my salute.

"At ease," he said, taking the cigar from his mouth. "I'm Captain Brooks, Special Services. You box, Autry?"

I tucked my cap under my left arm and came to parade rest, my feet apart, and hands behind my back, eyes forward, focused on a spot on the wall above the Captain's head.

"You look like you've never been hit," he said. "You Italian or what?"

"Irish/Indian."

"You could be European. You ain't French. You black, Autry?" he asked, as his rheumy eyes studied mine, for any reaction. "You afraid of them? We've got a lot of blacks in this program."

"No sir, I am not afraid of them. I don't really know any blacks, sir."

"How's that?"

Paul Ferguson

"Just how it worked out, sir."

"The Army's full of black men and women. You ever hear of our Texas president, George Bush, the black people's best friend?" He put the cigar back in his mouth. "Forget it," he said. "You want to be a sergeant?"

"I can't yet, sir. I haven't the time or grade."

"I'll decide that."

"Yes sir."

"I'm in charge of the Army's boxing program. I'll make you sergeant or any goddamn thing else I want. You understand that?"

"Yes sir."

"The Colonel wants you assigned to our program at Fort Bell. You want it or not? It means a stripe."

Special Services sounded good to me, like a cushy job where I would do what I like doing, training and boxing. "Yes sir, I want it."

"You people get younger all the time. I don't suppose that it will break your heart to be transferred to California, will it?"

"No sir."

"Don't get me wrong. It's hard work. We fight five three minute rounds and you'll train full time, and until you drop. Whatever it takes. And you train or you're out on your ear. You got that."

"Yes sir."

"Then we understand one another?"

"Yes sir."

A week later I received orders to report to Fort Bell, along with a notice I had been promoted to Sergeant, E-5.

Just ahead the sidewalk dead ended in a cul-de-sac blocked by a curved, knee-high safety rail. I stepped over the rail into deep brome grass and jumped a low ditch to walk up, through a scattered corps of branching saplings, onto the pitch dark parade field where I returned to a steady jogging pace. The sprouting nettle, sedge, and tufts of lumpy fescue made for rough footing, but the air was clear. The perimeter building lights hung jostling against the distant-dark beyond, the orange-yellow manmade suns, like castellated sky flares, silhouetting the end of the grassy field against the empty street. Overhead, cold stars encircled the universe and sky with an oceanic beauty of infinite quietude. Pioa, a Lakota, had different names for the stars, like what he called the Dusty Trail, Seven Persons, and One That Never Moves. By any name they were always the same, never changing, while changing everything.

If the Captain was on the level about, the program he presented – or if it had worked out like that – everything would have been all right, but I soon learned at Fort Bell it was not enough to be able to fight and win. Despite his boss's high opinion of my talents, Brooks considered me, at twenty-three, a spoiler, someone too old to start training for the ring and just good enough to ruin a serious fighter's chances. The Captain's opinion was no big deal. Officers were usually full of themselves, making excuses in advance of their own potential mistakes, and forced to live by excuses to cover for the incompetence of their superior officers. Brooks only mattered because he sidelined me, Pioa, and two or three others that the Colonel liked, but the Captain did not consider good enough for his team. He thought us dangerous to his own corps of hand picked fighters and reduced our chances of proving ourselves and the danger to his boys by reducing our chances of ever getting in the ring to meet and defeat or damage any of, what were known as, the Captain's 'glory boys.'

None of us were happy at being excluded, and like Pioa we all had our own ideas why the Captain would not let us box. In any case, he was in charge, unbeatable, and our constant nemesis. Otherwise, the training was good and so was the food, the best, all you wanted to eat, and if now, I was going to be allowed in the ring, I could not expect anything more. If it turned out to be a one time shot or some sort of trick, then I really wanted out, even if it meant reenlisting or more likely, in another six months, taking my papers and going home. The economy was good, but there were not a lot of job in Alabama. I did not actually have to worry about that. I could always make a living doing the high and dangerous stuff, building radio and microwave towers for my cousin.

Jogging now across the parade grounds I thought of being at home, the clean, warm air of the hill country, the endlessly green forests, the smell of sugar pine and Douglas fur, cedar, the huge, mossy oaks, and springy earth under the trees, cushioned with pine needles and deep leafy mold, the river, zigzagging through the wooded valleys, the sky like a deep blue blanket overhead. These were the sights, smells, and feel of home. I supposed if I had to quit the Army and returned with nothing more to show than my honorable discharge, it would be enough and more than enough if I never left the hills again in all the rest of my life.

Leaving the parade grounds I trotted along the lighted, empty streets to a narrow, paved road. The electric lines along the road buzzed in the dark with a cicada hum. I passed the last brick barracks and turned onto a sandy, sunken street closed with traffic horses and guarded by flaring smudge pots. The air was full of the pots' smoky, kerosene stink and soot. I entered the condemned labyrinth of two-story, World War II, wooden barracks. The tall clapboard walls were pale with the peeling plywood boards nailed over windows that once had stood watch under the peaked roofs, now silhouetted black against the stars above the incandescent pole-lights on every corner. Winged insects swarmed to the glow and spiraled down, broken from their failed flights of glory. Their winged corpses littered the broken, crumbing curbs in jaundiced pools. I heard, but did not see, a ball of fluttering feathers lift into the dark. The big bird's tenebrous shadow lingered corporally against the stars, appearing momentarily to follow me before silently drifting away. I knew it was an owl, but being alone in the dark with the gods did not intimidate me nor give rise to memories of denying they somehow bound a harmonious whole. In the day, in the presence of others, it was nothing to deny such things, but I was not the kind of Indian who changes in the dark; I simply was not superstitious, and did not believe any sign better than no sign at all. Anyway, the owl had not screeched or even hooted. Its presence would have been enough for Pioa to take a warning and turn away, but I could ignore it. If the magic worked, or seemed to work, causing Indian people to still identify with it, binding them together with it and to take refuge in it, for me at least, it felt like a trick with fate attempting to trap and freeze me in an identity a long time gone. No doubt the universe was a whole, one, but the starvation winters, the epidemics, the massacres, the pulse and pauses of a magic that enslaved peoples in their suffering and death, did not accurately foretell the story of the bloody rages rained upon them. If there were gods, they neither made nor manipulated the chaos with warnings or blessings. Rather, like the stars fixed in the firmament, they too were, forever silent.

Beyond the last crumbling barracks was the main drag. The traffic was heavy and I stopped, waiting on the corner for a break in it. In the distance cars were parked in the parking lot under the lights of the commissary. On the street behind the commissary a line of vehicles would be waiting with motors running to enter the already packed lot under the gym's spotlights. The fights drew fight-fans and families from base and – most importantly – the surrounding towns dependent upon the fort's payroll to afford this Friday night's diversion. I crossed, quickly, in front of an approaching pickup, noticing the driver's pale, blank face behind the glass, as I jogged along the shoulder, into the passing headlights.

I was not the only one arriving late. The fights had already started. The mostly male crowd was rowdy in a smoke filled blue atmosphere wired with an electric current like anything could happen. I felt the infectious rush of the noise and excitement in my blood as I pushed and dodged around the soldiers and civilians, standing in the back behind the already crowded seats of metal folding chairs arranged twenty rows deep around the ring. Stopping in the center aisle I stood looking beyond the seated fan's silhouetted heads and shoulders to where the overhead ring lights blazed down on the fighters. A bald referee, wearing a glaring white short sleeve shirt and black bow tie, followed around a stark white, flabby looking Murray in green trunks and some beautifully muscled black guy in crimson trunks. They were heavy weights. There was no super heavy weight class in these competitions. Anyone over 81 kilograms, 175 pounds was a heavy weight, expected to meet all comers, whatever their weight. This made for some interesting and strange bouts, but these two guys, Murray and the black, looked well matched, though Murray was outclassed. The black was aggressive, up on his toes, punching from outside, then getting close, catching Murray with a punishing flurry of body shots that echoed through the crowd. Murray would not be able to eat or keep anything down for days. He stumbled, and fell on the black in a clutch, tying the guy up, and deliberately ignoring the referee's orders to break.

Coach was there on his feet at ringside below Murray's corner. He was a little guy, wearing a green sweatshirt with ARMY writ large in white letters across the front. In his younger days Coach himself had been a featherweight. His gray, pummeled and scarred face was like a clay sculpture that under the lights melted, twisted, filling with shifting shadows as he jumped around, a grotesque elf, waving his arms, attempting to describe with his hands and arms the instructions he was hoarsely shouting at Murray.

The Captain also would be ringside in the seats reserved for officers. Murray was one of his glory boys, but Murray was no prize. Coach could not create a fighter, or more importantly make a fighter a champion. All he could do was work with a guy's own abilities, and it was Brooks or the Colonel who did the picking.

Murray attempted to rest on the ropes. He had a bleeding cut that was black above his left eye and what looked like a long crack at the side of face from above his eye down his cheek to his chin. He covered himself high with the gloves in front of his face, and the black came in low downstairs to his gut and went up as Murray dropped his hands, quickly sending a shot through the gloves into Murray's eye.

The crowd was on its feet, yelling for Murray's blood, urging the black on. This was why they came. The more blood, the louder they wailed. I lost sight of the fighters through the excited crowd's heads and shoulders. My own heart was racing. I anxiously wanted to be in the ring, thinking I could beat either of these guys. Maybe both at once. I turned away, one hand holding the fight bag against my hip as I impatiently pushed through the jostling bodies towards our locker room around to the left of the building. There was a visitor's locker room to the right at the far side of the ring.

I looked for Nina. She would not be hard to spot. She was special, different from most of the girls and women present with their ashen faces and stringy hair and to-the-point t-shirts, tattered above tight jeans. With Terry as her only parent, constantly moving from one Army base to another, Nina had raised herself. Now twenty-two, she was solid as a rock; tall, 5'9" – over six-feet in heels – with long legs. She was also ambitious for the good life, working locally in Marshall, selling television ads. She had style, a certain way of walking and dressing in the big city wear of heels and pin skirts with lacy, pastel blouses and the station's signature maroon blazer, her waist length hair pulled up, framing an oval face drawn to perfection with reds and browns and blues, chiseled from mountains and seas and dreams of dusky sunsets and applied by her to widen her eyes, sharpen her cheek bones, narrow her nose, and flush out her pale, caramel lips.

Navaho, her world had always been white, the wives, daughters, and women of the Army, and like them, although aware and proud of her native blood, she was as romantic and as nescient about Indians as any of the white girls.

She wrote poetry and touted a list of Indian women writers whom she admired and quoted. "These women," she told me, "have been preserved through generations of losses, betrayals, and deaths to challenge and change the world. They offer our people salvation. You men, your hearts are on the ground! You've made such a mess of it all."

When I had first arrived at Bell, before I knew what a drunk and moocher her Dad, Terry was, he invited me to dinner at his house in town. She was there, sitting across the table from me, so beautifully perfect that I could not look at her and breathe. I barely touched the food. She lived alone and I walked her home through the dark, tree lined streets. We must have talked, but I do not remember. We went inside her building, upstairs, before we reached her apartment I had picked her up, kissing her, holding her in my arms while she fumbled for the key to open the door for me to carry her through the darken rooms to lay with her on the bed. I could feel her hunger, matching my own, and her ravenous valley so hot and humid between her soft thighs that it nearly burned my fingers to touch her there.

She was my indecision about staying or leaving the Army. I could not believe she would return with me to Alabama, but it did not stop me from wanting her. Many nights I caught a cab or rode a bus into Marshall to sit on the hardwood floor of the candle lit apartment, drinking cheap, white wine that she bought in gallon jugs with screw tops, and listened to her while she breathlessly recited her poetry.

I was not a fair audience, but for her I was Indian, the real article, the legend made flesh, a warrior of the Kainais, The Many Chiefs. To me, watching her tender mouth move, her black eyes flashing, the rising, flickering flights of her slender hands, my thoughts engrossed in the taut rise of her heavy breasts, swelling with every uttered breath, stretching the frail fabric of her blouse, she was my desire incarnate, tightening the tension in my loins, so the words were lost on me. She was all the poetry I wanted or need. Her touch made me tremble and I thought often of it when we were not together.

I did not see her now and hoped she was present to watch the fight. I wondered if she had decided against coming, ironically, not knowing I was fighting.

I stopped outside the locker room. "NO ADMITTANCE," stared at me in stenciled black letters from the gray, metal door. This was the moment, but I did not know what to expect. Squaring my shoulders I pushed opened the door, letting it slam noisily as the drumming echo of the showers greeted me with the familiar humid miasma of heat and light, the smell of disinfectant, sweat, and sour towels, the harsh murmur of male voices.

No one seemed to note my arrival. Across the room Lyle stood watching his fighter Hanson, dressing in front of a metal, dark gray locker in the long bank of lockers built into the walls around the room. Turner and Dodge, like Lyle and Terry, were trainers, and they sat with their heads together on a bench near Hanson. Turner's fighter, Jackson was boxing himself in the mirror, warming up. Dodge's boy, Craig, robed, his hands wrapped, sat beside Dodge. Terry was in the middle of the room with Skull stretched out on the table in front of him. Behind them was a second, empty stainless steel table covered by a gray foam pad. Beyond this table, there was a wooden table against the wall with towels stacked on it beside the open arch into the showers. Buck's blond head and wet torso was just visible through the steam above a waist high, gray tiled partition.

I crossed to Terry. He was enveloped in the smell of wintergreen, rubbing it into Skull's heavily muscled back. Terry did not immediately look at me. Skull opened his eyes, and on seeing me, grunted, before turning his head away and laying it back down.

"You're late," Terry said in a gravely voice. "You seen the Captain?

"I just got here."

Terry was oddly proportioned with a big Navaho head, barreled torso and short legs. His flat, ocher colored face was etched with deep furrows and was puffy and sweating. Like the other trainers he was wearing green sweats with ARMY stenciled across the front. His underarms were darkened in wet circles with the ooze of his continuing relationship with bottled death. A towel was slung over one shoulder. He turned his big head and pressed his rubbery lips against it, wiping at the dripping sweat.

"You're in for Miller," he said.

"The Captain's pet," I said, surprised. "What's with him? He sick?"

"Yeah," Skull grunted. "Sick"

Terry shrugged "Whatever," he said.

Like the other trainers Terry was a utility man, a caretaker. He moved things along, and like them, he was strangely reserved, almost mysterious about Brooks and his machinations. He was so busy now not looking at me, working on Skull; it was obvious something was up.

Behind Terry, through the arch, Buck was out of the shower, toweling off, his back to us. His wide shoulders narrowed down into a V above round, snow white buttocks. The skin was blotchy, spotted, his back and shoulders red from the hot water. This was also how it was with Terry. He was full blood and neither white nor red.

"So you want to tell me who I'm fighting?"

"Coach will tell you."

"You tell me."

He absently licked his lips. "Krogstad," he said, still not looking at me. "Get showered."

My gut tightened. "The inter-service champ? The Krogstad who knocked out the Navy's champ? What's he weigh?"

"I don't know."

"Com'on, Terry. What's happening?"

He shrugged. "It's not personal."

"Why me? Why not Miller?"

Terry turned his head to look at me. "Its politics. Nothing to do with you. Get showered."

"If it has nothing to do with me why am I here?"

"Get showered."

I went over to the bench near the entrance and dropped the fight bag on the bench, then sat down beside it. The mood of the room was all wrong. At Bragg there was always noise and a certain camaraderie. It was fun. But there was no joy here, no bravado or esprit de corps, nor concern from the trainers to their fighters; these guys were solitary and solemn, seriously intent on their futures, and the showers' drumming echoed their intense fears.

The door flew open. Murray, robed, stood framed against the noise of the crowd behind him. His blood covered face looked like it had been chewed up and spit out. Doc, the cut man, and Barker, Murray's trainer, were supporting him. He lurched away from them as the door swung shut. Terry grabbed him and led him to the table Skull had quickly vacated.

Seeing Murray did nothing to raise the fighters' morale. He was a portent, a mirror of our own futures, an omen, as serious and as real as if someone had hung a noose from the ceiling.

Coach entered, banging open the door and slamming it behind himself. He ignored Murray and swept past me to the waiting trainers. He hissed through his sunken nose at Turner to get Jackson on deck. Jackson, already on his feet, joined Turner. Leaving them, Coach came back over to me. I stood up to meet him.

"What are you on, Indian time?" he asked, snorting what was meant for a laugh. The shaved, priapic top of his head barely reached to my chin. He reached up and squeezed my shoulder. "I'm kidding you, kid. We're all Army here."

Terry, wiping his face, came over and stood with us, facing me.

"What you think, Chief," the little man asked Terry, "He's a team player, isn't he?"

"Yeah, "Terry nodded. "A team player."

"Sure," Coach. "You're a team player. Yeah you are. A smart kid like you. You're all right. Bet you got a girl. Yeah, right? You give it to her good too, don't you? Good looking kid like you. Ahh, she can't keep her hands off you either. That's the way it is with you kids now days."

Terry knew, or should have guessed Coach was talking about me and Nina, but there was nothing in Terry's face or eyes that indicated he had heard.

"Hey, look at me," Coach continued. "I want you to listen now. You're in with the Champ. He's got the height and reach and weight on you. He's a big boy. I want you to stay away from him. All we want is an exhibition and you don't get hurt. If you get in trouble, let Chief here know, and he'll throw in the towel." He leaned closer, taking hold of my arm. "There's a stripe in it for you," he whispered, shaking my arm.

"Last time I heard that, I wound up at Fort Bell."

"No jokes," he said. "I'll joke. Listen to me Stay out of his way." He released my arm and put a hand on Terry's shoulder. "You can't beat the Champ," he said. "Just don't get hurt. Talk to him, Chief."

He started away, but stopped and looked around, his smoky eyes icy under the scar thickened brows. "It's the Captain's party. We don't want to ruin it for him," he said, turning back to join Turner and Jackson, standing by the door.

"I'm not supposed to fight him?" I asked Terry, trying to get it straight in my own head.

"I don't make up these things," he said. "You want the stripe?"

Before I could answer Hagie pushed open the door and stuck his red head inside the locker room. "Let's go!" he yelled. "Fight time! Let's do it!"

Doc hurriedly left Murray and joined the others at the door. Coach led them out while Hagie held opened the door, following them out, the door swinging shut.

"You better dress," Terry said.

I could feel my face burning, but could not think, and mechanically turned and sat back down. For a long moment I sat without moving, then finally bent down over my knees and impatiently jerked at my boot laces. I took a boot off and set it up beside me on the bench, then began unlacing the other boot. I had not done anything that should have caused them to believe they could involve me in their dirty politics.

"This is bullshit, "I muttered. The boot lace broke away in my hand. I stood up, staring in disbelief.

Terry was again beside me. "You're okay," he said.

"You believe in signs," I said.

I did not hear what he answered, but knew he was a believer. I went a little crazy, kicking the bench, lifting it up, sending it flying, slamming against the metal lockers.

"I came to fight," I said. "Nothing changes that!" I turned on Terry. "You think I would throw a fight? What did you tell them I am? That like you I'm a dog to trot at their heels? That I would do anything for another stripe? Maybe that I'm like these others, afraid of them? You think I'm scared?

He backed away and stopped with his hands on his hips, looking at the upset bench, "It's not like that, Jack," he said, wiping his face.

"What do you mean?"

He looked innocently around the room at the others, as if expecting them to explain. "Who said anything like that? All Coach said was to be careful out there. You can do that, can't you? That's all we meant. Be careful. It's the same for everyone."

"No, it not! Why isn't Pioa here? What about the others? It's not the same. It's Brooks and you. All of you, letting him get away with it!"

"We follow orders."

"Orders to throw fights?"

He looked worried. He seemed to stand thinking, holding the towel up against this mouth, staring over it at me. "Okay, Crazy Horse," he finally said, turning to walk to where Murray was sitting on the table, holding an ice pack to his face.

I looked around the room. They all knew what was up.

Skull walked over to me. "Do what you've gotta do, man," he told me. "I've seen Krogstad fight. He wants to get it over with right away. You've got to stay away from him. If you want to stand a chance, make him chase you. Wear him out. He never goes five rounds. When he gets tired, nail him good."

"What's he weigh?"

"He's three hundred. Maybe three-twenty."

"I weight two hundred and four pounds."

"Yeah?"

"What would you do?"

"Me?" he asked, laughing. "I wouldn't let him catch me. If he did hit me I'd hug the canvas."

"You a trainer?" Terry asked, still standing beside Murray, sitting on the table. "Let it go."

Skull nodded and went over to sit on the bench with Hanson.

"Don't be stupid," Terry said, looking at me. "Don't let him hurt you."

"I'll do what I have to do," I sighed. I had no intentions of quitting before I ever started.

The door swung open with the crowd noises flooding the room. Jackson and Turner entered, followed by Coach and Doc. We had lost the match, and Jackson was not happy about it. He did not look hurt, but spit blood onto the floor as he shook his head, loudly blowing blood from his nose. He went directly into the showers.

Coach came over to me. "You're up after Hanson," he said.

"Sure," I said. "Why not?"

I do not remember much about the next 25 minutes, except that I was in my trunks and Terry had finished wrapping my hands when Hagie opened the door for Hanson and Turner, again followed by Coach and Doc. Hanson had won, but he was the only one celebrating.

Terry and Doc hustled me out the door, following Coach up the aisle through the restless crowd with Hagie behind us. Doc was reputed to be one of the best cut men around, and was the one thing that was in my favor. The crowd roared their approval as the Champ entered the ring. He did not look all that big, at first, through the smoke and glare, but began growing the closer we came to the ring. By the time I actually crawled through the ropes from the apron and stood in the corner with Terry and Doc, I was staring at a blond mountain draped in white satin trunks with a black stripe down the sides nearly as wide as the yellow one trying to crawl up my back.

Terry had me step into the chalk box, getting the rosin into the rubber soles. The announcer entered the ring with the referee. I stepped out of the rosin and grabbed the ropes with my gloves, squatting and stretching. The announcer introduced me first with 6-0, win-loss. I turned and stepped out of the corner, my arms raised. There was a low nearly inaudible smattering of applause. They were saving it for Krogstad with his 31 and 2 win–loss record. As he was introduced they came to their feet, roaring approval. Terry whistled. I turned around to him, but neither he nor Doc said anything. Doc stuck the mouth piece in place as the announcer introduced the referee. He then thanked Captain Brooks and Special Services for the fine job they had done in bringing the fight card together. As he left the ring the referee called us out for instruction. The three of us went out to meet Krogstad and his seconds. He seemed to grow another foot wider as we crossed the ring. I was 6-2, and was staring straight ahead into his red chest hair and pale, freckled skin. There was a single drop of sweat, crawling bug-like from hair to hair through the freckles. He was not all muscle, and carried an awful lot of lard and extra weight around his middle. A hard shot to the gut with a sledge hammer might have brought him down, but I would not have bet on it. Or maybe if I caught him just right on the tip of the chin with that same sledge hammer – and was lucky – I might knock him out. This was fairly dangerous thinking. I did not want to make him mad at me.

I raised my eyes to look into his icy blues and it was a mistake. He was glaring at me, and I saw myself, reflected, moments away from being carried out of the ring.

The referee finished his instruction and told us to shake hands. Krogstad growled and turned his back without offering his glove. The referee grabbed him and brought him back. The crowd booed as we touched gloves. I felt a little better, knowing he was not infallible.

Doc led me back to our corner. He and Terry stepped through the ropes. Terry went down the stairs as Doc leaned over the rope, telling me, "Don't let him hurt you. It ain't worth it."

I suppose he meant well.

The bell rang.

I was still facing into the corner, watching Doc on the stairs, and probably in no hurry to start. It was a bad mistake to make.

Krogstad rushed across the ring, charging at me, and was on top of me when I began turning. The heat and force of him hit me like a wave, warning me in the same moment I saw his glove, coming in from way back, like a load of bricks meant for my mausoleum.

This was no time to think. I ducked and his arm whizzed by above my head, brushing my hair to keep going, and wrapping back around him. His shoulder twisted with a popping sound and he leapt up, and back, spitting out his mouth piece to yell in pain, grabbing at his upper right arm and shoulder with his gloved left hand.

The arm was obviously dead at his side. He turned and stumbled towards his corner. His people were climbing into the ring and standing along the apron, coming in through the ropes. The referee grabbed him, then turned him over to two others guys in the corner.

The crowd was on its feet, booing me. They thought I had somehow fouled the big man and wanted my scalp.

I stood back in my corner, bewildered, watching the action across the ring, in Krogstad's corner, not exactly knowing what was happening. There was a crowd around Krogstad. He was hidden, on a stool, in the corner, by their backs and legs.

Terry climbed into the ring with Coach onto the apron, shouting we had won. I had not thrown a punch and did not get hit.

"How?" I asked.

Terry grabbed my hands, removing my gloves. "T.K.O.," he said. "Looks like he dislocated his shoulder."

"I win?"

"Yeah," he nodded. "You're the Army's new inter-service champion."

"I'm the champ? Can I win the championship on a disqualification? Can I?"

"Yeah. Why not?"

The referee came over and raised my arm. "Krogstad," he said, "sprung his shoulder."

I pulled my arm down, free of his hand, and threw them both in the air, leaping up and down, bouncing on the canvas, shouting down at the audience members in the chairs beside the ring.

They were Krogstad fans and had come with him to watch their hero knock my brains out. They wanted blood and had shouted and applauded the loudest before the match began. I had upset their plans and the order of their universe without even throwing a punch. They were confused and angry; telling one another it was a fluke and was not fair. They did not get it, and never would. It was not fair, not to Krogstad or them or me, but fair had nothing to do with anything. It was reality and it was perfect! I had won!

I leaped up on the ring ropes to laugh and shout at them to go collect their winnings. They deserved to be taunted. Coach grabbed my arm and Terry had me around the waist, pulling me down to the canvas for the official results.

I could not quit laughing, during the announcement, and maybe was a little hysterical with the relief of still being in one piece. I had won by doing nothing more than being true to myself. Anything could happen. Brooks no longer seemed important. He had called me a spoiler, but he was wrong, and maybe I was also wrong about Nina, maybe she was just waiting for me to ask her to marry me. I had not been willing to quit the fight without trying and it should be the same for me with Nina. I had a feeling it was going to work out for us. I mean what-the-hey, I was the real article, and the legend made flesh, a Kainais' warrior!

Paul Ferguson

HAND OF GOD

This is a copy of a letter from my cousin, Sam S_
of Orville, Alabama. The original is in my archives
at the University of Alabama - Tuscaloosa. This is
where I come from and where I would be, if I had
stayed. I have corrected the spelling and added the
underlining…..

Hand of God

Robert,

From one prisoner to another I am locked up within myself by <u>your</u> God.

Excuse this writing. I never learned to spell. I am glad to hear that you are still alive, as we are all not. Earlie, Jack, Lish, James and their wives are all dead now (heart trouble). I have heart trouble. Mary's heart is bad for a long time now.

I am glad you may live to see the power of the Almighty. For in 2004 in the 7th month there is going to be an earthquake so bad it will scare some people to death. The volcanoes will shoot ash so far out in space it will go into orbit around the earth. The world will be dark with ash and move towards the sun. A hot wind will blow from the east all over the world. All ice will melt and the oceans will rise. All low lying lands will be underwater. One month later the moon will be bright as the sun and the sun will be 7 times as bright in one day and in that day the Lord will bind up the breath of his people. Then you will know <u>my</u> God.

Your cousin,

Sam S.

Paul Ferguson

Sam had his first heart attack in December, 1983, almost exactly a year from the day of my first heart attack, December 1982. He wrote this letter in January, to warn me of God's coming in July. Everyone loves Sam and I am no exception. Growing up we were hunting and fishing buddies. It would be easy to say I was Huck Finn to his Tom Sawyer (since I was the orphan in his Daddy's house,) but there was an awful lot of Huck in Sam. He never left the woods and river, except once to go up north to Carolina to fetch his Indian bride, Mary. He only recently learned to read and write, so this letter would have been written with great difficulty and great concern for my soul; and how elegantly he expresses the difference between us; founded in how we have dealt with the world that locks him up within himself and he would deny and destroy that which I continue to search out and embrace.

Mary died in June of heart failure. Knowing Sam, he is stronger than ever. With the loss of certainty in his God, and without Mary, the disappointment and 'taking away' of his wife are his just punishments for presuming to know God's will. They are in effect, the hand of God, and so Sam, with his faith intact, will probably live to be a hundred plus. It does not prove anything. I fully intend to be there to help bury him.

Paul Ferguson

THE HOLE

Everything I write is based on my experience, it is true. It's just a matter of telling it.

The Hole

There was a single, low wattage, red bulb in the close, narrow hall outside the cell's solid steel door. Every third day the bulb came on when a guard entered the hall. From inside the cell you did not know the light was on or that the guard was in the hall until he slid back the foot square slot at the bottom of the cell door and the red glare filled the opening.

The cell was three feet long, two and a half feet wide, and five feet high. The walls were painted a flat black and did not reflect the red light. There was no sink or toilet. No bed. No blanket to warm you. You were stripped and left naked in the dark twenty-four hours a day. You could not stand up or stretch out and could only sit huddled on the cement floor with your bare back against the wall.

You never knew who the guard was because you could not see his face through the door. He was not always the same guy. Some guards wore wedding bands or high school or Masonic rings. They were married and had children and were good neighbors in their community. They came to bring food and change the waste bucket and refill the water bucket. They did not speak and had different ways of demanding the buckets be passed through the slot, sometimes grunting or bending over to move their hands in the opening and sometimes banging on the door with their fists or kicking it with their shoes or boots. The buckets were identical, except for the smell, and some guards were mean enough to switch them, putting the drinking water in the waste bucket without cleaning it.

The food, a "juteball," made of cooked tomatoes and corn meal, compacted to the size of a baseball, was pitched through the slot to the floor. That the cell was full of cockroaches and that the floor was filthy with them, their dead bodies, and your own excretions and that it was not fit to eat off, did not matter. There was no other food. Nor did it matter how quickly or how slowly you ate, all at once or holding on to the ball and picking at it in small bits for the next three days. It was not enough to last or to keep your stomach from cramping with the constant hunger.

After a while you could dream, while awake, that the slot was open. Sometimes you would be asleep and wake up dreaming that the slot was open and the slot would be open. Your mind made the connection and after that you wanted to sleep all the time and wake up and eat, but could never be certain afterwards if the guard had come or not and you had eaten or if you had only dreamed it.

Eventually, they let you go, out of jail, back to the streets, stripped of whatever had still remained of your innocence. Or maybe it was just that you had found something out about them *and* yourself. Something you had never really wanted to know; something that rattled around, loose inside you, knocking against your thoughts. Either way, you could not forget it – nor could you forgive yourself for knowing about it.

Paul Ferguson

DREAM NO DREAMS

As long as there is a top, there has to be a bottom
to walk on.

Dream No Dreams

They ran us into the holding cell with me rubbing the red marks on my wrists. The handcuffs had hurt. The tank was already full of prisoners and we had to slide in among them. Those around me were black. I saw a first, then a second white face through the sea of black heads, but I was packed in and couldn't move. The guard yelled at us to be quiet – to hold and wait – then disappeared down the hall.

The wait lasted about an hour. A guard presented himself and directed us down the dimly lit hall to a big room full of running showers. The air was hot and full of steam, the bulbs in the ceiling like cloud-shrouded suns. I thought of a primeval world and its miasmic mists, a time when the sun was not even a dot in the swirling clouds. I was light-headed, and afraid of falling, so steadied myself against the wall.

The order to undress and shower was given. Naked, I made my way across the slippery floor. The hot water stung, reviving me. It felt good against my body and for the moment, I was saved.

The past twelve hours had been spent among the filth of sick drunks and shivering drug addicts in a tiny cell behind the courtroom. I didn't know what had happened to the others arrested with me. A white cop had shot an unarmed black man in Old Town. We had been picked up during the demonstrations. The cops had separated us. I had been charged with resisting arrest. In the courtroom, I had stood before the bench and pled guilty. I would have grown eloquent about it but the Judge had failed to ask if I had anything to say before sentencing me! He had simply looked hard at my shaved head and beard, coughed, and then mumbled something to the clerk at his side.

They wrote for a moment, flipping papers, and then the bailiff took me out. In the hall, as he opened the cell, I had asked him, "What now?"

He had looked at me as if I were stupid, "The County," he said.

"Jail? Don't I get a lawyer or something?"

He had shrugged. "Not for a misdemeanor. When the Judge coughs like that, it means six months. You're lucky. He don't like no one fighting his cops."

Lucky? I suppose I was – that he didn't have me shot – but six months in Cook County Jail! I went dizzy at the thought. It wasn't fair. I was demonstrating as much for the Judge as for anyone. Why hadn't he understood? Why hadn't I told him? But this was no good. The fact was, I hadn't said a word. I had missed my chance, and it was too late to start shouting about truth and justice for all.

My sole comfort was that I had resisted

arrest. At the time it had been important as an example to the others, now it seemed doubly important. It was all I had, and the thought of it soaked my wounds. I had struck at them and they hadn't destroyed me. Unless they did, I wasn't defeated, just simply out of the fight.

This all came clear as I stood in the shower. I was alive and young. I had my health. Sure, I was in jail, but I hadn't changed and wouldn't let it change me.

My strength returned, and as I left the shower, I suffered with patience being sprayed with their greasy insecticide, even though on dressing it ruined my clothes, causing chemical stains around the crotch and underarms of my pants and shirt. Dark circles that would remain and forever smell of insecticide. But I went ahead, seemingly unaffected. In fact only minutes later in a second room, somewhat smaller than the shower area, where we were lined up single file, one behind another to be photographed and fingerprinted, I dared to ask the guard photographing me how life was treating him.

He stood behind the camera and shrugged. "You home now?" he asked.

"What?" The question confused me.

"Nothing," he said. Keep your head up." The strobe lights on either side of him dimmed. "Next."

"This isn't my home," I tried to explain. "I'm not a jailbird. I was picked up at the demonstrations."

He pointed at the exit. "Through there and down the hall," he said. "Next!"

I turned away. That hadn't worked, but he could think whatever he wanted. I knew what was what. Still, in some way I knew he was right. For the next six months this was home.

I was depressed again and left the room dragging my feet. At the end of the hall a large holding cell stood open. About two-hundred men filled the tank and pressed their bodies against the walls and bars.

I had knocked around some since getting out of the Army: Los Angeles, old Mexico, Dallas, New Orleans, and now Chicago; and I had worked at just about everything, including – for a single day – a slaughterhouse, where the sounds of the cattle's helplessness had forced me to quit. These same sounds were in the hall, coming from the holding tank. I recalled how cows in the pens had cried, moaning pitifully to one another through the blood soaked air as they waited for the butcher's knife, which was always to come. Remembering it made me sick. I did not want to share the fate of the cattle at the hall's end. But I had no choice. I had to cram myself in among them.

I tried not to touch anyone, to pick my way through the carcasses and obstacles they represented, but they moved around, and around, going in circles, until at last I was disgusted, and angry with it, and impatiently wanted only to be out of the tank even if it meant being killed upstairs in the cellblocks – where, it was rumored-the jail's prisoners were burning one another alive.

I dismissed the whispers, though not necessarily their verity, by thinking of the dozen or more cell blocks throughout the six-story jail. I believed in luck, and with all that had already happened, mine had to improve. But if not, if things could get worse, I would do what ever it took to survive.

We were waiting for the warden to show. He had to admonish us as to the dos and don'ts of the Cook County Jail.

It seemed the middle of tomorrow when he finally stood in the hall before us. He was black, the color of soot, and wore a black tie on a white shirt with the sleeves pushed up to his black elbows. He had his hands on his hips and I could see the veins on his forearms. He entered the tank, frowning, making room for himself by shoving the men nearest him back with the rest of us. Then he stood glaring at us. When he spoke, his teeth showed white against the unfinished purple layers of his swollen lips. He spoke in a low growl. He said: "My name is Moore. If you don't know me, this is my jail. While you are here, we'll do things my way." The jail was all that mattered to him and he might as well have been blowing bubbles, talking to himself, his words bursting on his lips. I imagined a red-necked Sheriff, sneering, addressing a cell full of niggers. Or it might have simply have been Moore standing there talking to us, black and white, since prisoners are everybody's niggers, and Moore was no exception.

104

He might have thought he was top-cat in a cell full of cats, but there was nothing exceptional about that, as long as we were not his equals, we were cattle, and black or not, he was just another butcher.

When he finished, he nodded, satisfied with himself, and left us, a guard holding a clipboard took his place. He called out names: Brown, Green, Williams, Autry, and checked us off his list. In groups of four, me and three blacks, he sent us out to an outer hallway. A sergeant and four guards greeted us with a directive to strip.

I was beginning to respond on command. I stripped, stepping out of my shoes and dropping my clothes on top of them on the floor. A guard stepped in front of me. He ordered me to open my mouth and stick out my tongue, to raise my arms above my head, to lower my arms, to run my hands over my shaved head, to fluff my beard, to lift my balls; finally, to turn around and bend over and grab my ankles and to reach behind me, pulling apart the cheeks of my ass.

He kept me bent over, head down, ass in the air, cheeks spread apart until the Sergeant passed behind me and grunted for him to have me get dressed. The black beside me, wise to the process, was slower to obey. He waited until the exact moment the Sergeant walked behind him, then bent over and spread his cheeks.

Seeing my weary face as he was bent over, he winked, smiling as he mouthed "The official asshole inspectors."

I wondered who was degrading whom, and smiled, suddenly having to suppress the laugh I felt rising in my chest. I might appreciate the guy's humor, but the guards would not. I was not afraid of the guards. I did not think about them. There were just cogs in the machine to be cautiously watched and accepted as part of the system, but not to be taken personally, or to be made personal, giving them existence.

They stood idle, indifferently watching us dress. When we finished, the Sergeant jerked a thumb over his shoulder at an open door in the wall behind him. "Through there and up the stairs," he said. "You're assigned to G-3. Now move it!"

I followed the others past him, slowing to a near crawl as we entered the darkened stairwell. The shadows were heavy, filled with smells of cement dust, mold, and a strong ammonia stench of be-pissed corners. A narrow steel staircase with concrete threads twisted and turned, climbing six floors of sharp, skeletal angles between close cinderblock walls. Our feet echoed on the steps. Huge, green iron doors were lit at every landing by dim, incandescent bulbs, showing ghostly white letters and numbers printed on the doors: G-1, G-2, and another twisting twelve steps to G-3.

We gathered on the narrow landing. This was the end of our travels. The waiting cellblock behind the locked, green iron door, whatever waited for us, was home for the next six months, but I was almost too tired to care.

The strain on my companions' dark faces

was obvious. Eight out of ten prisoners in Cook County Jail were black, which said something about who they were and how they saw themselves and how they saw me. So, they knew what was happening, but I did not know how they would interpret anything I said. Like me, they were tired and scared and it was probably a good thing I kept my mouth shut and not provide a target for their fear. Besides, they did not look as if they knew anymore about what was behind the green door than I did.

I put my back against a side wall and slid down to sit on the floor. Closing my eyes, I waited for whatever would happen next.

I must have dozed. The sound of a guard, clinking up the stairs, the ring of his keys echoing, roused me. I looked up and he stood at the door, dragging it open.

Pushing myself to my feet I hesitated, letting the others enter. They quickly filed past the guard into the inky hole beyond him. I followed cautiously, resisting an impulse to balk in the door. It was as if I was about to step off an unseen ledge into eternity.

The interminable darkness engulfed me as the door clang shut. The others had not gone far. I stumbled into them. We were surrounded by the hard touch of iron bars on either side of us.

"We're in a hall," I said. "Go on."

Moving by feel, I followed them out into a long, wide area crowded with prisoners. A dim light glowed from a small, black and white television set on a small shelf in the far corner. The television emitted a low mumble, otherwise the room was quiet. The silent prisoners lay on the floor like so many black logs, or sat crowded shoulder to shoulder on benches attached to the sides of half a dozen wooden picnic tables, three tables on either side of the room. No one showed us any interest. We crowded together where we stood. I thought this odd, but supposed we were waiting to be told what to do,

A whisper hissed at me out of the dark, coming from among the men silhouetted at a table beside and just in front of us.

"Hey, yo, white boy!" White boy! Who you?"

"Jack," I answered automatically, seeing white eyes above a wide spread of white teeth, hanging suspended in the faint outline of a black face, the body and legs invisible in the surrounding dark.

"Do ya box, Jack?"

I thought longingly of the ring and year spent in Special Services as an Army boxer. The rules inside a ring were simple: No hitting below the belt. Not so in the real world.

"Yeah," I told him. "I box."

"Ya think ya box!" he corrected me, the smile widening, issuing a low snicker. "On G-3 ain't no white boys what box good."

Another man, a shifting shadow across from the speaker, leaned over to him and tapped the wooden table with his knuckles. "There ain't no rappin' Moe. Chill."

Moe turned away. I had an uneasy insight into the fear that could shut a man down like that and wanted no part of it. I sensed the others with me, having witnessed the exchange were just as uneasy. They inched closer together, moving away from me.

My eyes were adjusted and I swept the room and saw only shiny black faces in the screen's flickering blue light. Across the floor, centered in the back wall was a row of bars that opened onto a long, dimly lit narrow hall. The cells would be off the hall. With blacks running G-3, it seemed likely the whites would stay close to their cells, keeping out of the way. I could not imagine them coming to my rescue, no matter how white I was.

The television suddenly snapped off. No one went near the set. The screen simply folded into itself with the light vanishing. Everything went black, and then a single bulb came on overhead, turning the room a dingy yellow with heavy overlapping shadows. The prisoners scrambled to their feet to push and carry the tables to the sides of the room, stacking them on top of one another, clearing the middle of the floor.

The room's walls were actually bars

running from the floor to a ceiling of heavy iron plates with tiny stars punched through the metal. Green dust beams slanted through the holes, disassembling in the lurid light. Low murmuring rose as the men crowded together among the stacked tables and against the bars, hunting for a place to stand. My companions disappeared to join the others and left me standing alone. There was not another white face to be seen and the black faces, staring at me now, seemed openly hostile.

The largest black man I ever saw stepped out of the crowd and crossed the floor to stand stiff-legged in the middle of the room. He held up a hand the size of a catcher's mitt, demanding quiet. "All right, all right," he rumbled. "It's fight time." The prisoners roared their approval. "All right," he quieted them. "We got four fish." He waved indifferently in my direction, as if I was all four. "I'm Ross Barns, he said, looking at me, the whites of his eyes yellow in the dim light. "I'm barn boss. This your first time down? You been here before?"

I shook my head. "No."

"Uh-huh," he nodded. You could've got a worse tier. I only got one rule. Everybody boxes. You understand? You got to box. Who wants him?"

A general, eager shouting erupted, accompanied by waving, raised arms and stomping feet. I was a popular guy. The white enemy, but, if it was unfair, it was exactly as fair as everything they had been taught to live with. Here they were the majority, able to intimidate those who had oppressed them for being black and the minority. It did not matter we were in the same sinking boat, or that I was not the enemy and we could be bailing together to stay afloat. All that mattered was they were on top and as long as there was a top, there had to be a bottom to be walked on.

I understood, but it did not make them right. "What if I don't fight?" I had to repeat myself, shouting to be heard above the general clamor. "WHAT IF I DON'T FIGHT?"

The room instantly quieted, heads turning to look at Barns.

"What?" he demanded, obviously surprised. "You didn't hear me? Everyone boxes. If you don't, maybe we'll have us a weenie roast with you as a weenie. You a fag? You a bald headed sissy?"

I was not going to let myself be destroyed. "I was arrested in the protests in Old Town. The cops had to beat me up."

"You and a hundred others."

My heart lurched, jumping into my throat. This was the first I had heard of the others. "Where are they now?

He frowned, hunching his massive shoulders. "They set up a special court for them. How come you here?"

The riot must have made the TV news. "I was the first arrested. Was anyone hurt? Did they mention any names? What did they say happened?"

He shook his head, frowning. "I don't know 'bout all that. You trying to help a brother?"

"Trying."

"Yeah," he said. He studied me a long moment. "Ya still gotta box."

I glared at him.

He smiled, showing his teeth. "You don't want none of me," he said.

"No," I agreed. "I don't want to fight you. I don't want to fight anyone."

"I'll do you a favor. You pick him. I'll do that for you. Take your pick of the brothers."

"It doesn't matter." I was not afraid, but my voice sounded strange to me in my head. I cleared my throat, swallowing. "Anyone," I said.

"Anyone?" he repeated. "Anyone?"

"Yeah," I said. "It doesn't matter."

"It matters," he said. "Skinner, my main man. You want him?"

"Right on, bro," yelled the answer

returned from among the crowd. "I got 'im."

Skinner wriggled onto the floor from behind his friends and moved toward Barns. He was tall and thin, smiling, bobbing and throwing punches at the air. He looked more like a dancer than a boxer, up on his toes, drawing encouragement. I had at least fifteen, maybe even twenty pounds on him. I wondered what he knew, or if he was good enough to make up the weight difference, and how much of his act was show and bluff meant to frighten me.

Barns threw a friendly arm around Skinner's neck, pulling Skinner to him. "Skinner's tier clerk," he explained. "If you beat him, you get the job. Can you write?" I refused to be baited and he shrugged. "It ain't important. If you beat my nigger, I'll get someone to write for you. You get his cell and he sleeps out here. There ain't enough cells to go around. You got it?"

Skinner pulled away from him. "No shit," he said, laughing. "He can't get this!" He was again dancing, laughing, his buddies yelling encouragement.

"I got it," I said, adding to myself, "If you keep your word."

Barns stepped back among the others. "All right! Get it on!"

Skinner jumped at me. His fists spun around and over one another in some sort of fancy guard. It looked good, like he had style, but it did nothing to protect his face or body. I jabbed him twice, quick, then hit him with a straight right. The punch caught him below the eye, cutting his cheek and backing him off of me. I knew he knew he was in trouble – the way he pulled up his head, looking surprised, his black eyes losing their laughter – but his friends did not know. They urged him on, yelling at him to kill me. He seemed to have other ideas. He tried to move back as I stepped in, but his feet tangled and he was off balance. He had to drop his arms to recover. I saw the opening to his head and stiff-armed the eye above the cut. He twisted around, putting his back to me, then turned back around and stopped and stood with his arms down, staring at me. The eye was already swelling.

I thought he'd had enough. "You quitting?" I asked.

He raised a hand, touching his cheek, smearing the blood. He looked at his fingers. "You cut me!" he yelled, his face twisting.

"Quit," I warned him. "I can take you."

He swore at me, describing what he supposed was my relationship with my mom. Raising his arms, hands doubled into fists he turned sideways, trying to fight while keeping the injured eye away from me.

Flinging my left high caused him to flinch and duck, dropping down and towards me. I hit him with everything I had. My fist came up, crashing into his chest, sending him backwards into his friends. He threw up his hands as I set my feet, but he was too late. I connected hard to his face. The punch, while not all I intended it to be, was solid. His knees buckled and he sat down on his heels, his head cocked to look up at me with his good eye.

I saw he was finished and dropped my hands, wondering what would happen now. Would Barns keep his word?

Behind me, Barns yelled, "Come on! Clear the day room. Two minutes!" he ordered. "Skinner. You sleep on the floor."

Lock up. So I had been duped. No one else was expected to fight. They had wanted the white boy and had got him, except that I had won, earning a place on G-3.

The talker Moe appeared at my elbow. "Come on, Jack. I'll show ya where ya sleeps."

He was in front of me, black and small, chest high, already turning away for me to follow him into and down the hall. There were solid iron doors along both walls. "Jack," he said to someone, but when I looked up no one was there.

"This it," he told me, stopping and sliding a cell door back along the wall as he pointed through the opening into an empty room. "Ya sure can box! Ross Barns will run that worthless Skinner nigger off. See if he don't! We won't have no nothin' like that on G-3. I'm closin' the door now, Jack. Lockin' up. They'll be comin' to count soon."

Somehow, I was inside the cell, sitting on the steel
bunk, nodding at the closing door. A thin wool
blanket – no pillow or sheets – lay bunched on the
dirty, plastic mattress pad. The dirt did not matter.
I lay down and pulled the blanket over my head. I
slept then, exhausted, and dreamed no dreams.

THE EIGHT-BALL KING

My buddy, Leo Fugate, could sink the eight-ball on the break 99 out of one-hundred times. When asked how he did it, he would answer, "Practice, practice, practice."

My nephew named his son after my dad, Lucky, and Leo, and called him Lucky-Leo – claiming he named him for the two coolest guys he ever heard about. I suppose that makes them legend.

Of course this story has nothing to do with any of the above.

The Eight-Ball King

I used to be a stage magician. Mostly supper clubs. I loved it, or thought I did. Then I met Hank Meyers and he changed my life.

He was an older, nice guy, a little guy with a bald-head and a dark, rubbery face that sagged and looked like he was frowning even when he showed his crooked teeth in a smile. He managed the magazine kiosk on the corner of Las Palmas and Hollywood Boulevard, across the street from the Hollywood Lounge where we played pool. For the third time in a week, he bet me ten bucks I could not sink the eight ball on the break.

The bartender, Tommy, also bald, but tall and heavy set, his shirt-sleeves rolled up his hairy forearms, leaned on the bar, watching Hank rack the balls at the far end of the table; our bet, two crisp tens were under a shot glass at Tommy's elbow on the bar.

There were three of us, otherwise, as usual in the early afternoon, the joint was empty.

"Some guys never learn," Tommy said. "Hank, you're a glutton for punishment.

Hank shot Tommy a stubborn look as he lifted the rack from the table. "You stay out of this," he said. "Pal Joey won't do it for free. So how else am I gonna learn? Go on Joe, shoot."

"Just for you Hank." I said, lowering the stick to the cue ball as I bent over, taking my time lining up the shot.

"No, no," Tommy said. "Wait up, Joe. You gotta call the pocket."

I looked back over my shoulder at him, shaking my head. Then looked across the green felt at Hank. "Same pocket," I said, pointing to the left back pocket with the stick.

Hank nodded. "Sure. Go ahead Joe. Never mind him. We know were its going."

All I really knew was to aim and shoot. I liked telling admirers it was finesse, and maybe, on some instinctual level, it was. I had a feel for the shot, driving the cue ball hard through the one-ball, the three-ball, clearing the balls behind it, the cue breaking off the four, slicing the eight-ball into the corner, all of it happening too fast to see.

"Son of a bitch," Hank swore as the eight ball dropped into the pocket. "If I didn't see it, I wouldn't believe. Damn! What are you, fuckin' Houdini?"

"I'll tell you sometime," I said, laughing. "Soon as I get all your money." I dropped the stick among the balls on the table. "You know how to get to Carnegie Hall, don't you, Hank?"

"Don't give me that Carnegie Hall shit,"

he said. "I'm serious! It's a fucking trick. Tell you what. You can tell me. I'll give you a hundred bucks for it. I won't tell a soul. You got my word."

He followed me over to the bar in front of Tommy. I slid the bills from under the shot glass, putting them in my shirt pocket.

"Thank you, Hank," I said, smiling.

"Two hundred?" he asked. "Give Joe a drink, Tommy."

"Okay, one more," I said pointing at the round orange face of the big neon clock on the wall above the shelf of liquor bottles behind the bar. It was near two o'clock. Rehearsal began at three. We would finish around five, five-thirty. That would get me to dinner by six and back in plenty of time to set up for the eight o'clock show.

"Three hundred," Hank upped the offer. "We're friends. God damn it, you're a magician. You guys buy and sell tricks all the time."

Tommy sat the drink on the bar. "Give my friend Hank another beer," I said. "Put both drinks on my tab."

Tommy called himself a 'mixologist,' claiming he had always been behind a bar. It showed. I could barely taste the Rose's Lime through the Absolute. Obviously, we agreed completely, endorsing Fleming's insistence in the Bond myth to stir, not shake a martini. The advice served a gimlet equally well.

Hank had climbed on the stool beside me. He ignored the beer Tommy set in front of him. "This is it," he said. "Four hundred. What do you say? That's all I got."

Tommy laughed, snorting. "He's got more money than fucking Bill Gates."

Hank frowned at him. "Okay, you guys. Five hundred. That's it," he said. "You guys ever see The Hustler, the old movie with Gleason and Newman? With a trick like this, I could go on the road. You don't even need to play. You never play and you can retire. What about it Joe? Five hundred? What do you say?"

I slid off the stool, finished emptying the glass, and pushed it across the bar towards Tommy. "Let me think about it," I said. "You have a good day, Hank."

"You think about it," he said.

"I'm thinking," I said, not thinking about it. Of course there was a way to do it. Maybe with magnets. "See you, Tommy."

Hey, Joe," Hank yelled as I reached the side door pushing it open onto the sun drenched Las Palmas. "A thousand bucks!"

The door closed behind me, leaving me standing on the street. A thousand dollars! If I had walked into traffic, I could not have been hit harder! The world suddenly slowed down. I saw my life, and a big part of it was all the time, ever

121

since I was a kid, spent playing pool. Even then, I was good. The stick was like an extension of my own hands. Being a magician came later. That whole thing about magic, and I liked good clothes, dressing up, being on stage, the center of attention, the audience, the lights. What was not to like? But I would never be a great magician. On the other hand, I was a great pool player, and without knowing it, I had sort of pulled a rabbit from the table. I had a hook. Thanks to Hank, I now knew people would pay to see it and pay to play pool with me because of it. This was huge, great, an epiphany, and I knew exactly what I had to do.

By the time I closed the act, the big dollar billiard tournaments in Las Vegas were over. I spent the next months on the road, following local money, but the prize, the national television exposure was in Vegas. They were expecting me by then and it was no surprise when I won. Afterwards I opened a billiard hall in Las Vegas. There are seventy-two of them now in twenty cities. By the way, Hank works for me, 'The Eight-Ball King'. I figured it was only fair. He still hasn't made the shot and still thinks it's a trick. But he doesn't argue now when I ask him, "Hey, Hank, How do you get to Carnegie Hall?"

KLOOF

A story in no way based on experience? Funny about that. My cousin thought the world would end July 2004. (see "Hand of God" pg 91) Something he figured out, all by himself. He wrote me, telling me to prepare. My response was, "Thanks for the warning – will write you more in August."

His wife, who believed everything he said for over forty years, died of a heart attack in June, sparing herself the July conflagration. I sent a card but have yet to get a reply.

Perhaps he is no longer there?

Kloof

"Everything has a purpose on this earth, and all things fulfill their purpose — seaweed, dung beetles, parasites — without agonizing or questioning. We are the only part of creation that is blinded by desires and thus ignore our particular purpose, individually and collectively, and spend our lives in mad pursuit of nothingness"

Gottfried Llewellyn-Jones
Anatomy & Evolution of Universal Madness

A small man, thin with a gaunt, boney face, quick, black eyes behind black rimmed glasses, wide forehead and balding pate, Abe Pikatellus normally gave the impression of being nervous, but this was different. Pikatellus was sweating, sitting hunched in his chair with it turned around from his desk in the cramped 42nd Street office, so that he stared blankly through the dirt-smeared panes of the single, rectangular window. The brick and steel mountains of Manhattan obscured his view of the sky, the gray horizon of everything, except the empty eyes of row upon row of unreflective widows in the towering buildings across the wide avenue. Ten stories below, hundreds of thousands of people hurried like scurrying ants through the traffic and past the shops and the eternally waiting mounds of garbage, cluttering the curbs. He thought briefly about the destruction Mayor Lindsey was causing on the city and of bigger destructions looming far beyond the steel and concrete canyon.

Pikatellus could not see any of it without getting up from the chair, walking over to the window, opening it, and pushing his head out into the foul smelling, smoggy air, looking down on the rushing street crowds, and he did not have the strength to move. He was nauseous and nearly paralyzed by the fear of what was going to happen to him, not that it was his fault, In fact, the only difference between him and the rest of humanity was that he knew the universe was about to implode.

There was nothing to prevent it. No uncertainty principle to restrict the ability to measure position and momentum simultaneously, nor relativity, nor any perceptual argument about the nature of light, and no multi-universe to spin the reality of his calculations into an alternate infinity. Even the second law of thermodynamics with its balancing act of exceptions was of no help. Pikatellus had opened Schrödinger's box, and what he had found, was the end of everything.

Originally, seeing where his calculations were leading, he had thought them wrong. He had abandoned them, but there had been something about them, something in him, something magnetic in the perfection of the way they described the universe that had drawn him back for another look. He was, after all, only human. Besides, if curiosity killed the cat, hadn't he heard it said that it was satisfaction which brought it back to life? So, he had started over, thinking his calculations wrong, and again he abandoned them, only to be drawn back to check and recheck the equations, concerned he had overlooked the obvious, yet fascinated, unable to resist the Siren's call.

It was the doing, the challenge they represented, and not the results. He certainly hadn't thought of the consequences, although he had known well enough that once a thing was known, there was no way of unknowing it. Now, knowing the worst, he compared his efforts with those of the scientist who had built and tested the first atom bomb. Robert Oppenheimer, the Manhattan Project's lead physicist, could not be certain the bomb's test wouldn't catch the earth's atmosphere on fire and burn the world to a cinder. The test was never about the result, but about the bomb itself. Exploding it, whatever the consequences, was the only way to be certain about the effort. So be it. Pikatellus had felt the same way about his calculations. He had followed where they lead, not creating reality, but discovering it.

Actually, things had always gone his way. He was fifty-six years old, unmarried, and self-employed. He liked to say, he was an independent inventor. He had never wanted a wife or family, or personal or professional complications. He was perfectly content with his computer and graphs, satisfied in the knowledge he had overcome man's real enemies, so that he believed he would probably die happy, having provided for himself and his future with his apartment and office, and his ability to feed and cloth himself and to keep up appearances when he met with attorneys or marketing people, or on occasion manufacturers.

He could tick off on his fingers a nice list of patents, assuring he would never want for anything, but now of course, what was the use? There was no future, and anyway, everything he had ever done had been wrong, or if not exactly wrong, at least they had been based on knowledge, that at best, was skewed, or perhaps, if the lack could be explained, just not right. On the other hand, it was no minor fact his efforts had paid the rent, they had supported him even if now his calculations told him there was more luck than wisdom in his creations.

More than once he had doubts about an invention, a lurking suspicion, just out of reach around the corner in his mind. Yet he had wrapped up the project, declaring it finished, and sent the invention out into the world, closing his mind to any doubt. If he had not done that, not let go of it – whatever his suspicions about the imperfections – nothing would have ever left his office. He would never have finished anything and would have gone on forever tinkering with it until he got it right, perfect, the way he had gone on tinkering with these calculations, until finally there could be no doubts. They were perfect. The cat was out of the box, and there was no satisfaction in having freed it.

Pikatellus wiped the sweat from his face, closing his eyes. He remembered suddenly that he had wanted to be a math teacher. When was that? Years ago. When he had gotten out of college? He had all his hair back then, and no glasses, but living in the world of academia, subject to its demands and disciplines, the constant politics. He could never have weathered that reality.

Well, no one had ever accused him of being masochistically inclined, nor of being one of the crowd. No, not then and not now, even now as he admitted to himself that he was exactly what he was; just another one of the – about to be extinct – crowd.

Was it better to not know what was coming? It would just happen. No announcement. No warning. No long good-byes. No pain. And it was close now. He could almost feel it and braced himself in the chair, but of course, he wouldn't feel it. No one would feel anything.

He wished he didn't know. What was responsible? The supposed accident of all great discoveries? Did that even apply to his calculations? He had overheard a remark at a cocktail party at one of his attorney's homes. He had not wanted to attend the party in the first place, but had, knowing he would pay for it one way or another anyway and might as well at least get a free meal out of the process.

Crowded into a smoke filled room, hot, unknown, and knowing no one, except the attorney and his wife, he drifted among the other guests, picking up small snatches of meaningless chatter, his attention had finally been tapped when he'd heard a bearded, young, rather shabbily dressed fellow he took for a poet, expounding an explanation of quantum physics that had sounded like metaphysical nonsense. Curious, Pikatellus had asked his host about the man. He had been Aaron Johnson, a quantum physicist, head of nuclear research at Nu-Burrow.

Startled by the revelation, Pikatellus, shocked to be so out of touch, found himself compelled by the computer, seeking information he hoped would offer a context for Johnson's remarks. The math, which shut out so many, was no problem. If at any time Pikatellus was lost, it was only in amazement as he began to suspect the atom was indeed the last refuge that, at heart, was of metaphysical belief. They offered not only god, but also the devil, wrapped in biological and social schemes as mendacious as anything the Eugenicist's and Fascist's had foisted upon the world in the twentieth century.

What ever might have been sound in quantum physics had been exchanged for a gain of money and fame in a confusion of playing against reality, in favor of private and public illusions. Logic had been abandoned to follow the idealism of Kant and his revamping of Plato's belief in eternal truths, apart from and above man, and supposedly found in mathematical proofs. Pikatellus knew the geometry so many people innocently accepted and clung to as verifying these proofs, had long since been demonstrated as relative approximations, due, among other things, to the sensitivity of the inner ear to gravity. Einstein's Theory of Relativity had also undermined these "proofs," effectively destroying the faith one could have in mathematics. Einstein himself had used the less than scientific method of these eternal truths, along with his imagination, and Ernst Mach's dismissal of human perception, to formulate relativity. He had fit theory to missing facts, starting with assumptions the facts did not allow for, then proceeding to work backwards, and moving observation forward by the induction of general laws. The method had little in common with science, and was limited by what he could know at the time, and by what he accepted as true. Yet, when the atom bomb was built and exploded, apparently confirming Einstein's equation of $E=MC^2$, physicists, adopting the method in madness, began fitting theory to the missing facts, ignoring what did not fit by making distinctions in order to sever the parts from the whole, creating spaces and an infinitude of universes in constant reduction of reality. The natural outcome, as Einstein discovered – crying out in frustration that God did not play dice with the universe – was an inability to put the parts back together into a unifying whole. While claiming to know all the right equations, like all mystics, physicists were unable to fit them into long-term mundane reality.

Einstein's supposed nemesis, Niels Böhr, exploited the fields so called limitations early on, defining the inability to separate phenomenon, the effects of the distinctions observers brought to observations, and the failure of language to describe perception. The cornerstone of classical physics, the Copenhagen interpretation affirmed Böhr's assertions: "We are suspended in a language in such a way that we can not say what is up or down.", and, "Phenomenon must be stripped of related phenomenon to be described, even when dependent upon the separate phenomenon.", and "No elementary phenomenon is a phenomenon until it is a registered (observed) phenomenon." Einstein's plea to an unknown for an orderly universe, along with Böhr's certainty, destroyed reason and common sense, while those with neither, spun into an endless argument as to whether a tree, falling in the forest, would make a sound, if no one heard it fall. The mystics, quick to adapt to the endless possibilities of a universe of infinite universes, adopted the Obscurantism of classical physics, knowing there was no one who could challenge them, as there was no certainty. Besides, when it came to math, even the most rational people were willing to remain silent and leave it to the supposed experts. Physics was math dependent, and had the atom, and it didn't take the mystics long to realize the atom was the closest thing possible to a perpetual motion machine. They began to tear it apart, disassembling it one constituent at a time, handing the pieces over to the technology labs, along with billion dollar government subsidies. Given enough time, money, and labor, there wasn't anything the lab boys wouldn't attempt. A thousand, ten thousand, ten million failures, kept them working, and meant little as their tinkering revealed the possibilities of light amplification, and with it, not only the ability to emit radiation, but the ability to read discrete frequencies of electromagnetic fields, making possible the gee-golly wizard like miracles, the microcircuits of the modern world.

The lunatics had truly taken over the asylum. Theories, however convoluted, were imposed upon facts. It was not science, nor was it magic, but rather, the practice of science reduced to serendipity. Whatever the process: lasers, computers, bigger and more deadly weapons systems, it kept the subsidies coming. Pikatellus equated the damage done science with the damage Plato's idealism had done again and again throughout history, providing the mystics a place to stand, to indoctrinate countless others with

information of a journey without destination,
leading them to applaud and praise a labyrinthine
illusion of metaphysical nonsense.

Faced now with this and his own
calculations, Pikatellus regretted he had not
known, had really not cared to know until now.
Perhaps, like so many others who had spoken out
against the invasion of physics into other fields, he
would have just been another voice lost in the
confusion, but at least he could have tried. Now,
he was just lost, helpless, as was the world, waiting
for the end.

The law of conservation of mass – stating matter
and energy can be neither created nor destroyed
since they are one and the same in different form
– while unchallenged, had consistently been
proved wrong. The energy released and measured
during every atom bomb test for over sixty years
had produced the same result. Somewhere there
was a leak. An infinitesimal (not quite zero)
amount of energy had repeatedly disappeared.
There was no accounting for it, until now.
Pikatellus had found the missing energy. It, in fact,
had been destroyed, leaving a hole in what he best
described to himself as the fabric of the universe.
As more atoms disappeared the hole had widened,
the fabric separating, stretching, causing the tear
to move away from the source of destruction.
Earth orbited at 66,662 miles per hour. The Virgo
and other constellations traveled at 970,700 mile
per hour toward the Great Attractor, which itself
moved towards an unnamed clutter inside what is
called the Shapley concentration at 805,319 miles
per hour. The Milky Way moved at nearly 500,000
miles per hour. Galaxies moved apart at speeds

proportional to their respective distances, roughly 160,000 miles per hour. The speed at which the tear was moving had no upper limit, gaining momentum in relation to distance as it spread. At some rapidly approaching moment, the coherence, the enthalpy, holding the fabric – and therefore the universe – together would become incoherent. The galaxies would begin collapsing, plunging toward one another to melt together, creating a singularity, a tiny black hole, approximating the conditions existing at the moment before the big bang. The end might as well be a new beginning, but of course, before that happened, the earth would have joined the sun and Milky Way in their own chaotic destruction. There would be no warning, nothing anyone could do about a small man, thin with a gaunt, boney...

MIDNIGHT UNDERTAKERS

These guys hijacked me in Meridian, MS. They made a mistake. The next day they were in the hospital; I was writing about it. The Selma-Times Journal paid me $125.00 for the article, 1,500 words, titled "Shipwrecked." The editor asked me how I'd learned to write the way I did. I told him, "By having something to tell."

Unlike Jack Autry, "Shipwrecked" was supposed to launch an investigation which never happened. The cemetery is full of unnamed, undiscovered bodies. Or the cops were right, they conned me. Either way, it should have gone further than it went. Perhaps it's ironic?

Midnight Undertakers

Jack Autry, eyes closed, nodding through
the false starts of interrupted dreams, heard the
pickup's tires exchange the smooth, steady hum of
the grating highway pavement for the crunching
shell and gavel of a tabby road, but Autry was not
alarmed. The strangers, Doug, the pickup's driver,
and Doug's friend Billy, riding shotgun, had gone
out of their way, picking Autry up at the gas
station, driving him to Meridian to find him a used
tire in the darkened lot behind the Goodrich Tire
Store, and now, returning him to the gas station
where the attendant would mount the tire, sending
Autry on his way.

There was no reason to think them
trouble, or to think they wanted for anything.
They were clean, good-looking guys. Doug had
black hair like sticks, parted in the middle, framing
a bony face with dark eyes, a thin nose, small
mouth and pointed chin. Billy was blonde with
blue or gray eyes, but otherwise they looked
enough alike to be brothers. The were both in
their early-twenties and both were well over six
feet, towering over Autry at 6'2" in his western
boots, and they were dressed alike in white t-
shirts, designer, Girbaud jeans, and white Jordan's.
Or maybe Autry was impressed by the pickup
Doug drove, a 1950 flat head V-8 Ford short body
with a lustrous candy apple red finish. Someone
had spent a lot of money restoring it, which fit
perfectly the remark Doug had dropped about his

family owning the tire store. Or maybe it was because Autry, a steeplejack, had been away from home for the past two weeks, building a radio tower in Lake Charles, Louisiana, and on the road for the past five hours with at least another two hours left on the road before reaching home and was tired, so that, he accepted his good fortune without asking himself - or it - what was up. Like why Doug and Billy were out in the middle of the night in the first place, or how they had managed to show up at the gas station just when they were needed?

Instead, having not asked these questions, and being tired, and seeing nothing wrong with Doug or Billy, he placed himself in their care, so that now the sudden detour onto the tabby road as they were returning to the gas station did not bother him, nor did it bother him when the pickup pulled over to the side of the road and stopped. In fact, Autry was determined to get what rest he could and kept his eyes shut, resisting the disturbance, figuring whatever was up, Doug or Billy could deal with it.

Autry opened his eyes, and then reluctantly, and only after he heard the passenger's door open. Billy was gone, the door wide open, framing a deep, night-blanketed field.

As Autry straightened in the seat, the pickup's round headlights reflecting back off the white graveled road to light the cab interior with a yellowish sheen through the windshield, a heavy rattling knock of metal banging metal shook the pickup. Turning on the seat towards the open passenger's door, Autry looked over his shoulder through the cab's rear window. Billy, silhouetted black against the black sky, stood at the side of the truck. Leaning over the rail, he pulled at a nearly invisible logging chain in the shadowy deep of the pickup's short bed. The huge links hung over the side, dropping to the ground, shaking and noisily banging against the truck.

It was no way to treat the antique's lacquered finish, but it was not Autry's truck, nor his paint job, nor his worry. He turned in the seat to Doug, who suddenly shoved his forearm against Autry's shoulder. Pushing Autry hard, Doug was intent on knocking or forcing Autry off the seat and out the passenger's door. Autry's two-hundred pounds was not so easily moved.

"What are you, crazy?" Autry demanded.

Twisted around behind the steering wheel, Doug held an open pocketknife in his left fist with the dully-silvered blade just inches in front of Autry's face. Autry moved back from the knife, scooting across the seat, letting one-foot drop outside the passenger's door.

"What the hell," Autry said.

"Get out," Doug hissed. "Get out of my truck or I'll cut your goddamn head off."

With Doug encouraging him to exit by jabbing the blade at the air between them, Autry slid off the seat into the night. Billy was waiting. He stood back away from the door, holding the logging chain waist high in front of him with both hands. The half-inch thick, five-inch long links were matted together in shadows, so that the chains looked like a long blacksnake. Billy swung one end of it at his side, the longer end coiled in the grass at his feet.

Autry moved away from the pickup to stand facing Billy with a distance of maybe four feet between them. The only sound was the idling V-8. The night was cool and the grass wet with dew. The pickup's headlights, reflecting off the road, were reflected back from the field at their left by what Autry took to be scattered black boulders. To their right across the road, along the shoulder, the headlights painted the drooping, leafy branches of thick woods with long black shadows. There were no stars in the sky.

"Is this a robbery?" Autry asked.

"Don't you move," Billy warned.

Autry nodded. "You're making a mistake," he said.

"You're the one done that," Billy sneered. "You don't know us. We're the Midnight Undertakers. We could have killed you while you were sleeping in the truck. You must have been born stupid."

Autry was no longer tired but was wide-awake. He was not scared or intimidated, nor particularly worried about getting hurt. As a steeplejack, he risked his life daily, was no stranger to dangerous situations, did not doubt he could handle whatever these guys thought they were going to do to him.

"Listen," he said. I'm wearing new boots with riding heels. They're not made for walking. I've got one hundred and sixty-five dollars on me in cash. It's all yours' with out all this bull. I'll give it to you for a ride back to the gas station. Just leave me the tire and we'll call it quits. Nobody gets hurt. You don't want to do this."

"Who said we're robbing you?"

"What then? Come on, man. You're a rotten liar. What are you going to do, leave me out here? That's stupid. It isn't funny."

"You ain't going no wheres," Billy said. He hefted the short end of the chain, as if feeling its weight.

"You're not listening," Autry said. "I'm making sense here. Take the money. Why got the police involved. You won't like jail."

"You can't hear good, can you? We got money. You think we're white trash? The only place you're going is in the ground with them others."

"What others?"

"They're all around you," Billy scoffed. Can't you see them?"

"My wife is expecting me in the morning. If I'm not home then, she'll have the FBI all over you."

"Shit," Billy snorted. "The law ain't going to bother us none. What do you think the FBI can do?"

"Just take the money and leave me."

"Ah, gee," Billy teased. "I thought you couldn't walk in them new boots.

The V-8 rolled over to tick in a guttering ping of cheap gas before stopping. Doug shoved open the driver's door, the gravel loudly crunching under his feet. He had switched hands with the knife and held it in his right hand with the blade down beside his leg, so that it flashed menacingly in the headlights as he came around the front of the pickup.

"God damn you, Billy," he swore, walking past Autry to stop beside Billy. "You going to kill this son-of-a-bitch, or what? We ain't spending all night at it."

Billy shrugged, "He's a smart ass."

Doug turned to face Autry. "Maybe I should do it for you."

Autry moved back a step. "Maybe not," he said. He raised his hands, palms out, as if to ward Doug off. "Hold up," he continued, "I want to show you guys something. He wore a long sleeved, western, cotton shirt with pearl snaps and reached to the breast pocket. Undoing the snap, he fished out a dollar bill. "You guys haven't seen this," he told them, stretching the bill between both hands, holding each side edge with thumbs and forefingers, to snap the bill with a loud pop. He popped it again. "It's no trick," he said. "Listen, when I drop the bill. It disappears. It vanishes. Gone. He snapped the bill. "Just like that."

Billy shook his head. "I seen it before. You pull it up your sleeve."

"No, no," Autry assured him. "It's nothing like that. This is the real deal. The real McCoy. It disappears. It's magic."

"Magic?" Billy repeated.

"Magic," Autry nodded.

"There ain't no magic," Doug said, incredulous. "We ain't as dumb as all that." He brought the knife up, pointing it over the bill at Autry's face. "You're trying to shit us."

"No. It's like I said, it disappears."

The knife worried Autry less than the chain. He could hit Doug, but not before Billy swung the chain, and it looked like he would have to take out the nearer, more aggressive Doug before he could hope to grab the chain from Billy, but then Billy bumped over against Doug to mumble something Autry heard in a blurred whisper.

Doug lowered the knife. "There ain't no way, dummy," Doug sneered. "He's shitting you."

Paul Ferguson

"No, no. I'm not shitting you," Autry said, his tone, he hoped, sincere. "Listen, I'll tell you what I'll do. You're both good guys. I'll show you how to do it afterwards." He shoved the bill out between his hands, holding it at arms length. Snapping the bill, he lifted it. Moving it back and forth in front of them. "Its real money," he said, snapping it again, then again. "No trick. Just keep your eyes on the money. Watch it now.

Doug shook his head. "Billy," he warned, "this ain't right.

"Go on," Billy said. "Go on, do it."

"Nothing up my sleeve," Autry said. "Now watch closely. Keep your eyes on the money."

"Let it go," Doug ordered.

"Keep your eyes on it."

Autry suddenly could not remember when he had last slugged anyone. There had been fights, plenty of them in his thirty-two years, especially when he was younger, but that was then, and even a baby could hurt you. These guys were not babies. They were big and real, real big, probably bigger than anyone Autry had ever faced, that, and there were two of them.

"Okay," he said, opening his hands.

The bill hung in the air, suspended, barely moving as it turned slowly, face down, to fall like a

143

wafting autumn leaf.

Doug and Billy, their eyes on the money, lowered their heads. Whatever doubts Autry had disappeared, vanishing as he moved, crouching, knees bent, dropping his right hand to close in a tight fist. He brought the punch up in a long roundhouse with all his weight behind it. The fist passed inches in front of Doug's startled face to smash Billy's jaw, jarring Autry's arm all the way back to the shoulder. Doug leaped back, turning to run, but Billy did not move or even grunt. Autry could not believe the blonde was still standing. He stepped into Billy, grabbing and jerking the chain away from him as Doug disappeared into the shadows beyond the end of the truck.

Billy, dazed, shook his head to clear it as he staggered towards Autry, reaching out with his right hand for the chain.

"No, you don't," Autry told him, raising the chain's short end to swing it up and back down across the top of Billy's head. The blonde collapsed like a sack of potatoes, blood splattering in Autry's face and down the shirtfront. Billy did not twitch or flop around. He did not move at all. Autry stood frozen in a vague moment, believing the blond dead, unable to make sense of it.

Still holding the chain, Autry stepped back from Billy. He heard Doug returning and looked up as Doug rushed at him, slashing the air between them with the knife. Autry swung the chain, releasing it in Doug's direction. The heavy links barely grazed Doug's wrist, but it was enough. Doug dropped the knife, howling as he clutched his hand and arm to his chest, jumping up and down, dancing with the pain in a circle and swearing at Autry.

Autry felt nothing for Doug. "You aren't hurt," he said. "Billy's dead."

"You killed him!" Doug yelled. Lowering his head, he charged Autry, screaming, "You killed him!"

Autry sidestepped the charge to swing at Doug's lowered head. The punch had little effect and Doug simply changed directions and slammed his head into Autry's chest and stomach, wrapping his arms around Autry's hips and legs to lift him up and push him backwards into the side of the pickup.

Pinned against the truck, Autry was surprised at Doug's strength, the strong arms and big hands, the bony shoulders shoved hard into Autry's face. Grabbing a fist full of Doug's hair, Autry yanked Doug's head around and smashed his hand down, butt first, into Doug's nose.

Doug screamed in pain as he released Autry and tried to twist his head free. Autry, releasing Doug's hair, stepped into him, locking his hip into Doug's side to flip Doug up into the air onto the pickup's hood. Doug grabbed Autry's shirt, holding onto him, dragging Autry with him.

The hood buckled noisily as they hit together and rolled across it to separate and fall off into the road with Autry landing on his feet, standing over Doug, who laid in the shell and gravel, on his back, his legs drawn up, lashing out in an effort to kick Autry and keep him away.

Kicking his legs, Doug attempted to scoot on his back across the road by twisting his body, now digging his elbows and shoulders into the sharp shell and gravel. Autry, more confident now of his ability to handle this big man stepped around Doug's flailing legs and grabbed them at the knees, forcing the legs together and down to pin them against Doug's chest. Autry lay bodily on Doug's legs, balancing himself by digging his own booted toes into the graveled road and using his weight to keep the legs folded against Doug's chest. With his own hands free, Autry rode on top of Doug's folded legs, hooking long, hard, roundhouses at Doug's head with Doug swearing and yelling, covering his head with his arms.

It did Doug little good. The steeplejack's steel-hardened fist beat and pushed Doug on his back through the cutting shell and gravel and across the road to the shoulder where they slid together sideways down the wet, grassy slope of weeds and bushes to the tree line where Doug managed to escape, rolling away, leaving Autry kneeling in the weeds, watching as Doug jumped to his feet.

For no more than a split second Doug hesitated to glare back at Autry, and in the headlights, reflecting off the road, Autry saw the swollen face with its bleeding nose and mouth and pointy chin and the t-shirt below the bloody face, hanging in strips like red flags. Then Doug turned and ran, disappearing into the velvet darkness of the woods behind him.

Autry pushed himself to his feet, but did not give chase and ignored the sound of Doug thrashing around through the trees. Winded, Autry stood doubled over with his hands on his knees, supporting himself while he caught his breath.

Doug came out of the woods some way up the road. Lit by the pickup's headlights Doug made no attempt to return to the truck, but hurried away, disappearing up the road into the waiting wall of midnight shadows, his footfalls coming back, echoing from among the trees along the weedy shoulder where Autry still stood, hands on knees, attempting to recover his strength.

II

Autry's dew soaked clothes were streaked with blood and grass stains and the knuckles of both his hands were skinned, though not bruised or sore. He straightened his back and felt a nagging stitch in his side as he walked across the road to the pickup. He thought of the pickup as part of Doug's trap now and did not like the idea of Doug possessing the antique Ford or possessing anything that tricked people into trusting him.

Opening the door, he leaned into the cab to look for the key. The dash switch was empty and he flipped down the driver's visor, then bent and felt under the seat and found nothing.

Frowning, he backed away and walked around the truck to where Billy laid on his back in the grass. Black blotches covered his hair and face and the white t-shirt was soaked black and was darker than the grass beneath the body. Autry doubted Billy would have a key to the pickup, and in any case did not want to go through his pockets or touch the body. Seeing the chain, he picked up the near end. He liked the familiar feel and smell of the ferric iron. He draped the chain behind his neck, wearing it like a stole with the ends hanging down to drag the ground on either side of him as he started up the road.

The white road faded to gray in front of him in the dark. The shell and gravel were uneven under foot and the chain was heavy and jarring, chaffing against the back of his neck as he walked.

The headlights soon grew dim behind him. There were no stars above as the dark closed around him in a heavy silence broken only by the crunching echo of his footsteps. He had read, or perhaps heard, that eight-hundred-thousand to a million people disappeared in the United States every year. The figures had seemed high at the time, but if it could almost happen to him, he was willing to accept the numbers, and even supposed the actual number was probably higher than what was being officially reported.

He had picked one hell of a place to break down. From its earliest days of riverboats to the present, Mississippi had a long history of hijacking travelers. Few states were as notorious as Mississippi for its ignorance and brutal poverty, but in fact, he had no one but himself to blame.

He should not have been alone on the road at night in the first place or have loaned the new Ram's spare to one of the other guys on the crew with a Dodge, nor should he have trusted absolute strangers to help him. Of course, he could not have known a flat would leave him stranded on the two-lane 80 East, west of Meridian at the only gas station opened within miles, or that it would not have a tire to fit his Dodge rim. The kid attendant had said he could get Autry a tire from Meridian in the morning. Until then he was welcome to park beside the station and sleep in his pickup overnight. He had just settled down when Doug and Billy had shown up, approaching him in the pickup and offering to sell him a tire. Autry had figured the kid attendant had phoned them. It had not seemed significant at the time. Autry was grateful and had not been particular about details. He had willingly accompanied Doug and Billy to Meridian; waiting with Billy in the pickup parked in the dark street while Doug disappeared into the lot behind the Goodrich store then almost immediately reappeared with the tire Autry needed. Autry, satisfied, had paid them, taking a folded roll of bills from his shirt pocket to peel off a twenty. Flashing the money like that probably invited disaster. It seemed now he had not done anything right all night. No matter. He needed to find a phone and report what happened. He imagined walking up to a strange house, knocking on the door, waking the inhabitants, all snug and cozy in their warm beds with their sweet dreams, to tell them of this nightmare.

    Up ahead the road swung sharply left. The dark grew grainy, tiny shadows slowly spreading in the shell and gravel. He looked left through the woods and saw headlights flickering between the tree trunks. He was still operating on adrenaline and his stomach tightened with a hollow jumpiness. He had not forgotten Doug had preceded him, and he did not like the way the headlights seemed barely to crawl along the road. It reminded him of spotlight hunters he had seen and knew growing up: A rackety old pickup, creeping along a rough timber trail, lights blazing on top of the cab, the periodic, odd rifle crack or ka-boom of a shotgun, echoing through the dark to make anything alive in the woods suddenly very dead.

He thought about hiding, but did not see how he could squat out of sight in the trees when he needed help. He would have to risk standing in plain sight to flag the vehicle down. He resisted an impulse to hurry into the lights and walked slowly over to stand on the shoulder along the boulder-strewn field. He shook the chain off, letting it fall in the grass behind him. If there was help coming, he did not want to frighten it away.

He watched the lights slow progress. It took a long time for the vehicle to finally round the curve, the light flashing in Autry's eyes as it suddenly stopped, the tires sliding loudly crunching the shell and gravel beneath them.

Autry estimated there was ninety to a hundred feet of road between him and the headlights. Since whoever was in the car could obviously see him, he stepped back onto the road, moving away from the shoulder, but hesitated, stopping to raise a hand up to shield his eyes.

Through the blinding lights, he recognized the glinting chrome bumper and grill of what he took to be an old Chevy, another antique.

The car roared, rocking, its lights dimming, then brightening with surging power. The rear tires spun in the tabby, slinging shell and gravel. Autry, the image of the boulders filling his head, leaped for the shoulder to fling himself – in a tucked roll – down the slope and into the field. He hit hard, his back slamming into something very hard and low and flat beneath him. Ignoring the pain, he pushed himself to his knees, his eyes wide, raised to the level of the road above him.

The headlights swept past, followed by a bulky silhouette. A spark flashed in the vehicle's interior, illuminating Doug's face through an open back window. A second face was beside Doug. Instantly, a popping report echoed across the field and back across the road in the trees, sounding as if Doug had fired three successive shots, instead of the one shot he actually fired.

Autry watched the taillights until the angle of the sloping shoulder blocked them from view. Doug had help and was armed, but obviously was more interested in retrieving Billy and the pickup than in chasing Autry, at least for the moment.

Autry's lower back hurt from whatever he had hit and he sat down on his heels and felt in the grass around him. Finding a rectangular stone facing – a foot across and eighteen inches wide – with sharp edges. His fingers traced the surface and found indented letters carved in the stone. A second stone pillow was beside the first. He moved and felt for and found a third, then a fourth stone. They were in the dark all around him, and what he had thought boulders were probably sepulchers, burial vaults, or monuments to the dead.

The field was a graveyard.

The discovery had little effect on him. Billy had said they would bury him with the others. These were probably the others. It made a sick kind of sense. A graveyard was certain to be deserted at night, making for a perfect killing field. He could no longer doubt his murder was intended from the first moment he had pulled into the gas station. The kid attendant had set him up, phoning Doug and Billy, and it probably was not the first time. They were too calm and organized. Billy had probably meant, "the others," the gang had killed. They were obviously a gang. Counting the kid at the gas station and the two with Doug in the car, there were at least five of them. Maybe more. How many people had they killed and what did they do with the bodies? He remembered hearing of murderers burying their victims in freshly dug cemetery graves, even of murderers who put their victims in freshly dug graves before the caskets were lowered, so that the bodies were buried under the casket. There must have been other ways to decrease the likelihood of the victims being found, but Autry was no investigator and did not need to worry about it, or complicate his thinking. He needed to stay focused and find a phone.

He walked back up the slope and found the chain, then, dragging it behind him, started down the road along the shoulder. He could barely see the pickup's headlights with the car's pink-tinted taillights stopped beside it on the road. He moved closer and saw a stick figure silhouetted black and thick against the lights. The silhouette wavered and disappeared. Almost immediately a shout echoed through the trees. A long silence followed while Autry stood and stared, watching for movement in the lights. All continued quiet. Then a door slammed. A minute or so later the stick figure again quickly crossed the headlights. He supposed it was Doug. He had probably carried Billy to the pickup or the car. It was all right with Autry if Billy was still alive. Autry had not meant to kill Billy or anyone, and dead or alive, Billy was no longer a threat.

After another long moment, the pickup's lights flickered, and then swung across the road to maneuver through a U-turn, pulling up behind the car. Autry congratulated himself on seeing it was a black or maybe dark blue 1952 or 1953 Chevy. A white antique plate in a chrome frame mounted high on the trunk reflected the pickup's headlights. Autry was too far away to read the plate, but would be able to describe the car to the investigators. The antique car, like Doug's Ford, would be known in small town Meridian. They were probably members of a state antique car club and would not be hard to find.

The Chevy moved away along the road with the pickup following close behind it. The taillights dimmed, and then disappeared into the dark.

Autry dragged the chain links into a pile

at his feet. Doug had returned in record time and might have other friends up the road who could be waiting for Autry. His best bet seemed to be to turn around and follow Doug. Maybe Billy was not dead, and Doug was taking him to a hospital. Civilization, the police. The town with some kind of help would be back down the road.

With the chain again draped over his shoulders, across his neck. He started down the road. He walked a long time. Although nowhere near as long as he thought. The chain, the night, the surrounding black wall of trees gave no indication of passing time. He thought he must have taken a wrong turn somewhere as the tabby turned to clay under foot. The high Cuban boot heels were no problem, but the chain became more burdensome as he struggled under its weight, stopping frequently to lift it off his neck and shoulders to drag it along behind him.

He thought of his wife, Nikkie. They had been married five years and there were no children, but they had four cats, three dogs, and two beautiful Arabian horses. They often rode the horses in the forests surrounding their home. He missed Nikkie's company when away and missed riding with her, the dogs, and sometimes even the cats running along behind the horses. He never seemed to have enough time at home and thought it a good thing Nikkie had her own career, selling real estate. He had phoned her before leaving Lake Charles and she would be expecting him by morning. He would have to call her again when he found a phone.

In his efforts to keep moving his thoughts

became a walking dream of snuggling with Nikkie in their big comfortable bed. He could hear her voice quite clearly, and although it was pleasant, he knew it was all wrong. He realized he was dreaming, sleepwalking. His eyes shut, and he opened them with a start to find himself staring into the charging Ford pickup's blinding lights as they raced toward him.

There was no time to think. He could already see beyond the headlights to the hood's smooth glass-like finish and the windshield's black glare. Ducking his head, he lifted the chain and heaved it, leaping aside as the pickup sped past.

He landed in the wet, knee high brome grass and rolled over in time to see the pickup's taillights disappear. They had not slowed, and if the chain had done any damage, he could not tell. He pushed himself to his feet and stood looking down the road. Doug could just keep coming back until he got it right and killed him. So far, Autry had been lucky, and while he never discounted luck, he did not think luck by itself without anything more was enough, and he had thrown the chain away.

He stepped onto the road and walked along it, looking for the chain. He did not find it and a wash of doubt engulfed him. Doubt was always bad in bad situations. He had seen men panic and freeze on towers when losing faith in themselves. He had talked his fair share of steelworkers into making the first move that would free them from their doubt and allow them to climb down a tower under their own power. He had also seen them freeze and refuse to move, so that he had to pry them loose, rigging up slings and falls to lower them to the ground. You could work towers all your life, and then, look down once too often, seeing yourself vanish in a smear of reddened earth, and have the doubt take you, if not killing you, then finishing you on the steel, so that you knew you were no good afterwards, to yourself or others as something you always thought you had was missing from inside you. He had it in spades, but he had to do something quick to take back the situation, if he intended to keep control of himself.

He moved without picking a direction and went down off the road through the brome grass into the trees. The ground slid down along a hillside of clay earth that was slick under his feet. Leafy vines hung down from the trees and caught in his hair and clothes and soaked him through and left him bone cold and shivering. He could not see more than a few feet and he stumbled often and hung onto the vines to keep from falling and they tore at his hands. He fought through a tangled thicket of small trees and thick brushes and found himself on level ground that was part of a narrow path along an earth bank. The road was above beyond the trees at the top of the bank and he followed the path, not wanting to get too far from the road. He was not too cold to notice his fingers were sticky when he touched his face. He could not find where he was bleeding and decided it must be sap from grabbing and breaking the vines. He felt better and safe, knowing he could not be seen and discovered by anyone on the road.

He followed the narrow path for what

seemed like a long time and had stopped to rest, leaning with his back against the dirt bank when a faint, scratchy static reached his ears. His heart jumped in his chest as he caught his breath, straining to listen. It was static and words and came from above him. He climbed the bank, using the roots to pull himself up and over the top into the woods along the road. Through the trees, he saw headlights, then crouched down in the knee-high grass, waiting, as they approached. A burst of static reassured him and he abandoned caution and ran out into the road to stop in the lights waving his arms and shouting for the patrol car to stop.

The car stopped and the doors on either side opened and two heavy-set deputies climbed out. They were slow moving men in tan Stetsons and gray gabardines with wide black belts strapped around their considerable waists. They came around in front of the car and stood close beside Autry on either side while he began telling them about the midnight undertakers and the graveyard.

The deputies grunted in ways meant to encourage him, assuring him they were listening and he needed to continue. He could not seem to get it all out fast enough and a lot of it was garbled and sounded like babbling even to his own ears. He worried the deputies might think him hysterical, but he knew what had happened and he stiffened against repeating himself or retreating from his story as they began questioning him.

"We had reports of gunshots," one of them said. "It's this fella, Doug, you say, with the gun? He the one doing the shootin'?"

Autry nodded. "In the cemetery."

"Yeah, okay. But if what ya say happened, he probably carried the other boy – Billy, that right? – to the hospital. Wouldn't ya say?"

"Yeah, but --"

"Ya got any objections to goin' along with us to the hospital?"

"No, no. I'll go." Autry was not certain Doug was at the hospital or had ever been there. "I don't know if they'll be there."

"Huh-hu," the deputy nodded. "Ah'll worry about that."

They walked Autry around on the driver's side and opened the back door, putting him in the backseat behind a wire mesh. They climbed into the front seat. The driver flipped on an overhead light as he picked up the dash mic, calling the county dispatcher. The partner sat with a clipboard in his lap, his pen scratching across a yellow incident report.

They were older men in their mid-fifties with gray hair, sideburns and round, ruddy faces. Autry expected deputies to be younger, but decided older guys would probably be better, with seasoned years of experience between them. He told them everything and they would know what to do. He did not know what more to say and sat back, staring out the side window, as the patrol car began moving.

Meridian, population 41,000, was five minutes away. The patrol car bumped through a dozen railroad crossings onto a narrow iron bridge over a black river and cruised into town along shadowy, deserted streets. On every other corner caution lights hung blinking against the dark above empty intersections. The black pavement looked wet with the reflection of the yellow lights. The curbs were lined by heavy, massive oaks in front of boxy wooden houses. A three-story, red brick courthouse occupied a central square of patchy grass at the center of downtown. Beyond the courthouse, infrequent lamps lit the indifferently littered streets. Ratty canvas and metal awnings hung above glass storefronts on crumbling façades. In a weed filled lot, an old car sat on tireless axles, its windows smashed, the square body bent and rusted.

Autry spoke up, pointing out the Goodrich store where he had waited outside with Billy while Doug had retrieved the tire from the lot behind the store. The deputy grunted, nodding at the information as he made a left turn. The hospital was in the middle of the block, two blocks down in a dimly lit three-story brick building. The cruiser stopped in a circular drive at the curb in front of a high concrete stairway that led up to a modern entrance of double glass doors in a back wall of a covered porch surrounded by a low brick balcony.

Autry refused the deputies' offer of medical attention. He felt dirty and tired and in need of a shower and his own bed, but otherwise was not hurt. They shrugged at his refusal and left him sitting, locked in the backseat. He watched their wide backs ascend the stairs and disappear across the porch, but it was all he could do to keep his eyes open and he leaned back into the seat and was soon asleep.

III

The slamming car doors woke Autry as the deputies returned and settled themselves into the front seat. Turning in their seats to look at Autry through the wire mesh, they took turns, with much grunting and head nodding, to explain Billy was inside in bad shape, jaw broken, skull fractured, but he would live, although he would stay in the hospital until he was well enough to transfer to the county jail. The other boy, this Doug had brought Billy to the hospital. He had been alone, but they would catch him, and anyone else who was involved.

The deputies seemed friendlier, obviously pleased with themselves, joking as they elaborated on Billy's confession, the patrol car driving away from the hospital. Autry gathered they had tricked Billy, and thought it funny, describing how they told him he was dying and needed to get right with God. No, he had not named Doug, saying, seeing how he was dying; he could not turn on his friends. He had said, however, it was all the friend's fault. It was all the friend's idea. They wanted Autry's new Ram and used the tire as a ruse to size him up and make certain they would have the right tire once they dumped Autry in the woods and returned to the gas station for the Dodge. They had not meant Autry any harm, believing that by the time he walked to a phone they would be long gone with the Ram. No, Billy did not know anything about a blue or black antique Chevy. He did not have much of a memory after Autry hit him, knocking him out. He did remember, they had not tried to kill Autry, and had only threatened him to get him out of the Ford pickup. It was Autry who had nearly killed them.

Autry was not buying any of it, but could see the deputies were satisfied. "What about the kid at the gas station?" he asked them. "He phoned them and set me up."

The deputy driving shrugged. "They a conned ya, didn't they? They lied to that boy too, Jimmy. Probably paid him for calling them to sell you a tire. It sorta figures, don't it?"

"It figures," Autry said, too tired to explain what the deputies should have known. "They said there were others. Told me they were going to kill me. They took me to a graveyard. They meant to kill me."

"They were tryin' ta scare ya," the driver patiently advised him. "Ya know? It sorta got outta hand. That's it. Ya all leave it to us. These things take time."

"We'll get to the bottom of it," the partner added. "Ah can promise ya that much."

Autry had leaned forward, anxious for whatever they could tell him, but now leaned back, away from them, his face flushed with burning warmth. He saw what was happening. The deputies were locals, talking about local boys. Whatever he, an outsider said did not matter. The truth was what ever the deputies decided, and they had already made their decision.

The car swung around the courthouse square and pulled to a stop in a narrow, paved lot in front of a two story gray stone building in the middle of the next block. The deputies got out and opened the door for Autry. He followed them up the flight of cement steps through a glass door into a large office. The deputy who had ridden shotgun handed Autry a pencil and paper and told him to sit at a metal desk and write a full account of what he remembered. He was to be as factual as possible.

While Autry wrote, the other deputy introduced himself as Phil. He asked what size tire Autry needed. Autry told him and Phil nodded and left the office. The remaining deputy stood a few feet away leaning with his right elbow on a short counter across the front of a room. A dispatcher in a room somewhere further back in the building kept confusing Autry's efforts with his broadcasts, his voice emitting a nasal whine as it echoed down a short hall to enter Autry's head. There was something about an abandoned car. Autry wearily ignored it and struggled through his statement.

He wrote on both sides of the paper, but skipped a lot of what happened in order to fit it all on the page. Finishing, he read it over, noting he had provided good descriptions of the Ford and Chevy, and he had included his belief Meridian was literally crawling with midnight undertakers. He nodded to himself, but then frowned as he signed the statement.

The deputy pushed off the counter and lumbered over and took the paper and stood beside the desk reading Autry's statement. Autry watched the heavy face under the hat. The teary blue eyes beneath hooded lids, following the words. The deputy grunted, his thick lips parting, drawing back to show yellowed teeth.

"Someone might think from this we don't know our jobs," he said, his eyes still on the paper.

"They might," Autry nodded, not knowing exactly what the deputy might be referencing, but never the less agreeing. "It's a gang," he said, "Five. Maybe more. They're killing people, travelers, and burying them at the cemetery. That kid at the gas station sets them up."

The deputy shook his head. "Ya don't wanna go around talkin' that way. Ya're only makin' trouble for yaself. 'round here there only two kinna people, them that's related and them that ain't. Ya don't know who's what sometimes. Ya think 'bout it," he paused, continuing to study the page, not looking at Autry. "Ah retired here after twenty years in the Army. Ya wouldn't know it, but this is a good town. A good place to raise a family with good folk. We don't kill people."

"You know who they are, don't you?"

The deputy's face whitened. He looked at

Autry, but immediately turned away. With his back to Autry, the deputy laid the paper on the counter. "Com'on," he said. "Ya'll wanna git goin'."

Autry followed the deputy out of the building. With the deputies keeping their mouths shut, it did not matter if Autry was right or what he thought he knew. There was nothing he could do.

Phil was already in the gray patrol car behind the steering wheel, waiting on them. Autry slouched in the backseat behind the wire as the pulled out into the street. The dispatcher continued calling, filling the speeding cruiser with his static-broken twang. The empty, shadowy streets zipped past and it seemed only a few minutes until the bright lights of the Bronco Station sprung out of the dark countryside to light the night.

The silver Dodge Ram was exactly where Autry had left it parked at the side of the low, white-tiled building. Phil swung the cruiser into the station and nosed in beside the Dodge and stopped. He opened his door and got out, walking past Autry's door behind him, expecting Autry to scoot across the seat to exit. Autry shrugged and slid over and out of the car and stood beside the Ram with the deputy. He pointed at the flattened left front tire of the Dodge and Autry nodded. The kid attendant was nowhere to be seen. Phil, who had opened the trunk, closed it and came around the patrol car, carrying a tire against his hip.

"Ya'll need this," he told Autry, smiling

broadly as he leaned the tire against the side of the Dodge.

The tire was new, a white pricing label pasted against the black treads. Autry was surprised and grateful. He had imagined himself being abandoned at the station to wait until morning when he would be able to purchase a tire from town.

"What do I owe you?" he asked.

Phil grinned, exchanging a look with his partner. "Hell, we've got county funds for this sorta thing," the partner said.

"Sure," Phil agreed. "Ya'll wanna git home to that wife you got waitin'."

The kid attendant came from around the corner to the front of the building. He could not have been more than seventeen and was thin and blond and dressed in dirty, dark blue coveralls. "Uncle Phil," he said. "Ya all got him a new tar?"

"Boy," Phil said. "Ah wanna talk to ya."

The kid smiled, showing a gap in the upper teeth. He then looked surprised, his mouth dropping open as he pointed. "Lookit there!"

The Ford pickup, its windshield smashed in, had turned in from the highway. It screeched to a tire squalling stop behind the patrol car. Doug, wearing a clean, white t-shirt and jeans threw open the door and leaped out. His face was cut and battered, the left eye purple and swollen shut. He ran up to the front of the cruiser and pointed a finger at Autry, "That's him!" he shouted. "That's the one right there! He smashed up my truck!"

The deputies rushed Doug. He did not look surprised and did not resist as they lifted him off his feet to lay him down on the black apron beside the patrol car. With his knee in Doug's back, Phil took the handcuffs from his belt and locked Doug's wrists behind his back. They then stood him up and padded him down. Finding nothing, no wallet, no comb, no money, they led him over to the patrol car, opening the rear door and helping him into the backseat.

Autry bent down, looking through the side window at Doug. Apparently, Doug's rage had abated the moment he had been arrested. He looked calm, sitting back, chin on his chest, his swollen face hidden in the shadows. He did not look worried.

Seeing him in cuffs did not mean much to Autry. There were others who were just as guilty. On the other hand, the antique pickup offered some little satisfaction. The chain Autry had thrown had not missed and not only shattered the windshield, but had busted out the right headlight and left long dents in the grill and across the hood. It must have made Doug crazy to see it, but it was now the pickup Autry thought Doug deserved.

Autry felt dirty. Asking Phil directions, he left the deputies standing with the kid beside the patrol car and went around to the front of the building and into the office to find the restroom. It was small and filthy and smelled of urine. There was no mirror. Just a sink and a toilet. The bowl of the sink was buried under black layers of muck and grease and there was no hot water. Probably no water heater. Autry did what he could, scrubbing the dirt and blood from his face and hands with cold water. He then used nearly a roll of toilet paper, drying and wiping himself clean. He was not so tired now, though it seemed like days ago he had first pulled into the station, asking about a tire. He wanted to get on his way home as quick as possible.

He returned to the Dodge and saw the kid jacking it down, the new tire already mounted and ready to roll. He did not offer to pay. He thought the kid one of the main ones involved with Doug and he glared at the kid, watching him roll the hydraulic lift around to the front of the building.

Phil came over as Autry unlocked and opened the Ram. Phil said the kid, Jimmy, had confirmed Autry's story of being picked up at the station by Billy and Doug, so there was no problem. The kid, he said, was a good boy. His nephew, actually. His sister's boy. "Ya know how it is. He had nothin' to do with it."

"Yeah," Autry said, wondering, if the kid was Phil's nephew, were Doug and Billy his cousins? No wonder Billy had not been worried about the police. "You'll take care of it," Autry said with veiled irony.

167

"Ya can be sure of that."

Phil's partner called out from the far side of the patrol car, asking if Autry would be back to testify. Autry nodded. Phil said not to worry about it. He expected the boys would plead guilty. There would not be a trial and no reason for Autry to return. Phil would let him know.

Phil held out his hand. Autry hesitated, but decided it did not mean anything. They shook and nodded and Autry climbed into the Ram, shutting the door.

It felt good to be back in his own truck on his way home. It was only another two hours to Orrville. He thought he could make it with no problem. He started the motor and backed the Ram out and swung it around the battered pickup. In his rearview mirror as he pulled up to the edge of the highway and stopped he saw Phil join his partner at the side back window of the patrol car. They looked like two dumpy old cowboys with their hats and gun belts. Doug's face appeared between them in the window. He had rolled the glass down and was leaning out. The kid walked over. They gathered around in a semi-circle, facing Doug, their backs a wall in Autry's mirror.

Autry imagined he heard them laugh. He could not be certain. He did not want to know. He had a wife at home, a good job. None of this was his real life. He pulled onto the highway. The patrol car, wall of backs, and red antique pickup, were all lost in the shadows as the station's lights faded behind him.

Paul Ferguson

EVERYTHING THAT'S COOL

The stage adaptation of this story earned a P.E.N. Award, this time for drama. It may not have the same impact as the play; I can not begin to judge it – knowing the ending.

Everything That's Cool

The jumble of plates, bars, and exercise benches scattered around the fenced weight lifting lot on the lower yard was deserted, washed white by a blazing overhead sun, the iron nearly too hot to hold, except for Red, lying on his back on a bench near the front gateless entrance, doing butterflies, a thirty-five pound dumbbell in each hand, and Big Cee, towards the back, squatting five hundred pounds, Cee's coal hauling punk, spotting him.

Red never intentionally missed a workout, rain or shine, and now, eyes closed against the sun, he silently counted, lifting the weights up and out, away from his chest, straightening his arms, bringing the dumbbell back, elbows bending, tattooed arms, shoulders, neck, chest, -- heart --, pumping with the strain. Up, out, away, and back, and again, and again, his oxygen starved muscles burning, begging for the last rep of the last set, and then he added one more, just in case he had lost count somewhere along the line.

Finished, he opened his eyes, squinting against the glare, letting the dumbbells roll from his fingers, dropping to the loose gravel cushioning the area. Sitting up, he straddles the bench as he uses the tail of his already soaked denim shirt to wipe his face. With his peripheral vision he saw Big Cee, his sweating black face swollen red, nose flared, eyes bulging, squatting under the weight, the punk, standing aside, arms akimbo, dark circles under deep set, unnaturally bright blue eyes, his narrow, ashen face drawn with concern, an obvious admiration for the big black's prowess.

Red deliberately ignored them. He, personally, was indifferent to their existence, although conscious of the relationship. He even admitted to himself he envied the affection, the caring and sharing, he had seen between guys like them. A third of the joint was blatantly homosexual, with the administration and guards ignoring, or perhaps encouraging them, and another third was flip-flopping in the dark night of their cells, hiding it, pretending, during the day on the yard, to be solid. The percentages were probably higher, since he had no way of actually knowing who was doing what with whom, but it was not a dance Red would do, or had ever done. He could take care of sex for himself. As for the other, he had been working on that, and it would depend on how things played out this afternoon with Wheeler.

Red glanced up, checking the white orb's position in the cloudless sky. He looked older than twenty-six. His long, brown-red hair was greasy, shiny with the sun, and slicked back from a tanned bronzed face with bushy, black eyebrows and hard lines etched to close gray-blue eyes above a blunt, cocked nose and wide, fleshy mouth surrounded by a long reddish mustache. He was a Biker and had been raised up north in the rough country above Shasta Lake by Biker parents in a Biker Community. The sun was all the clock he needed.

The guards would open the sally-port gates at four to let in Wheeler and the other trustees working outside the prison wall, but the guards could be counted on to run late. It was three now. Maybe a little later. That gave Red forty-five minutes to an hour to collect Boiler and Skinner. He hoped they would not have to whack Wheeler. But that was up to Wheeler.

Red stood, stepped over the bench, and went out through the gapped fence onto the lower yard. The volleyball court was directly in front of him. He crossed the sand, ducking under the net, going toward the basketball courts. The courts were crowded, and he quickly passed the noisy blacks along the outside of the near court. The flat smack of the balls, being dribbled on concrete, echoed around him, not fading until he reached the sandy half-mile track. The track encircled a huge oval of dormant, yellowing grass, dotted with gathered groups of usually two or three prisoners, but up to four or five, mostly white, sitting together or sunbathing with towels or blankets spread on the grass. The suits were big on recreation programs, and there was a G.E.D. class, and a computer repair class with sixteen students and a two-year waiting list, but otherwise, there were few jobs and no educational programs for a population of over 5,000 prisoners.

Red turned left on the track, moving in a straight line. Over his shoulder, behind where the track curved around at the bottom of the hill, a long, concrete ramp snaked its way up the hill through the dusty rocks and weeds to the upper yard where stone. fortress-like cell houses stood silhouetted like huge black blocks against the white sky. A jogger in a t-shirt and shorts passed Red as he left the track and went along a narrow strip of dried grass, paralleling a graveled rise to the macadam road. The road ran beside the prison's back wall. The walk was built of sandstone blocks and was sixty feet high. It ran for three-hundred feet before opening up and the road made a ninety degree turn through the opening into a walled cul-de-sac, containing the sally-port.

Fifty yards ahead of Red, Boiler and Skinner sat in the grass, waiting for him. They stood, nodding, joining and following him along the rise onto the narrow road towards the cul-de-sac. Red was heavier and darker than either of them and was taller than Skinner, but not quite as tall as Boiler. There were all dressed alike, in Biker grunge, the sleeves cut from the blue denim prison shirts, the jeans filth encrusted and too big, so that they walked on the legs, the rags of the cuffs hooked under the heels of their heavy work boots. They were all in their mid-twenties with long hair and mustaches and beards of sorts, and looked older, and they were all painted, more or less, black with a mixture of boredom and white power fantasies, tattoos of ink and ashes, flaunting skulls and demons, fierce dragons and naked women, swastikas and barbwire, stabbing Vikings and ghostly Klansmen, drawn in blood and belief for the ethnocentric aberrations of a mythological knighthood. Skinner was the only one to speak, swearing, wiping the sweat with a bony hand from his weasel like face.

The air was hotter in the cul-de-sac, trapped between the walls, and smelled of tar. The only gun tower, a railed, white box with tinted dark green windows and a low sloping red roof of weathered shingles, high up on top of the wall, and midway between them and the sally-port gates, cast a shadow on the grass at the base of the wall. The guard, Ledbetter, was no problem, and Red headed them for the shade to stand with their backs against the wall, watching the sally-port, the sun's glare causing the gray iron bars of the gates to waver and melt, bleeding into one another.

There was no other way for the trustees to enter the prison and every few minutes the iron gates at the far end of the sally-port would bang open on the outside road, admitting a pick-up truck full of trustees in orange jumpsuits. Wheeler would be among them. He worked as a gardener at the staff homes built into the hills surrounding and looking down on the prison, and it was this, along with the fact that the fat man was an ex-judge, a rumored child molester, and a notorious snitch, that had started Red thinking about him. Wheeler came and went from the prison and had access to what Red wanted, and the fat man could not afford trouble with Red. Wheeler had been on the inside of the system, running with the big boys gotten himself arrested for fixing cases in his own courtroom, and then had struck a deal with the Feds to turns state's evidence against his friends, prosecutors, defense attorneys, and other judges, naming names. Mostly, the friends had known enough to keep their mouths shut, and one way or another had wiggled off the hook, the system they refused to expose, taking care of them, which is what it would have done for Wheeler, if he had not panicked and had kept quiet and had not scared everyone. His snitching had reduced a possible three-hundred year sentence to a deal for five years, but the way Red figured it, Wheeler had not been meant to survive prison. The judge, sentencing him, instead of sending him down state to the park barracks to spend time playing golf and marveling at how pleasant life could be behind bars, had ordered the fat man sent to maximum security. Obviously, his former associates had not forgiven him. There were a hundred cons on the yard who knew who he was and would kill him for no other reason than to watch him die, and there were ten times as many who would do it because he was a snitch and probably a child molester with any excuse more than enough to get them to do it. So far, Wheeler's luck had held. He had three years done on the five and would be released in another six months, but if he come up dead, Red knew the suits would not look too hard, nor launch an investigation that might lead to the outside to Wheeler's former associates. The suits based their careers on building the system and would not knowingly create a scandal to tear it down. They have no compassion for the taxpayers and even less for the prisoners whose existence they depended on for their own existence. They caged and warehoused and premeditate and carry out executions of other human beings without knowing or having any desire to know if the people they caged and killed were actually innocent or guilty and thinking about that would get in way of the overriding joy of knowing they were doing their job, convincing themselves they were protecting peoples freedom and lives by caging and killing people effectively showing people killing is wrong, but the isolation of warehoused prisoners and the white room and quiet needle in the arm made it all to easy to enjoy the coffee and sandwiches served at the parties afterwards, the guard volunteering for the death squad for an extra fifty bucks, knowing it made no difference. With or without his help, someone would do it, the meat wagon rolling from death row to the county morgue at least once a month with one, sometimes two, and once, three dead offenders; add the ten to twenty prisoners killed on the yard every year by other prisoners, and another dead prisoner, even an ex-judge, would hardly raise an eyebrow. There was nothing to get excited about and too much at stake to let it get out of control. Millions of dollars were spent every year housing, feeding, and clothing prisoners, many hundreds of millions more were spent to build new jails, courtrooms, and prison warehouses, prison payrolls were the sole support of whole communities, and so everyone, one way or another, somewhere along the line was on the take, profiting from the prison boom, and they all had their hand out, the caught and the uncaught, the only difference between them and Red being that, Red knew what he was doing and was awake.

He looked up at the sound of the tower door above him opening. Ledbetter came out of the tower and leaned his khaki covered fat gut over the metal rail, shouting down at them, "Get away from the wall!"

Red saw Skinner start and look up. Boiler stepped into the sun, shaking his head. But Red did not move, except to fold his arms across his chest. Ledbetter was not even the regular guard. At Red's request, the Bikers had moved him from the mess hall to the tower. He could be counted on to look the other way. When it was over, he would be returned to the mess hall. The move had gone through the Captain's Office. Nothing happened inside the prison the Captain did not know about. He bragged that if there were three convicts on the yard together, one of them belonged to him. He always knew what was happening, usually before it happened. He probably wanted Wheeler dead, or maybe only thought Wheeler's former associates wanted it. The Captain was nothing, if not an opportunist.

"Hey, come on," Ledbetter shouted. "Go on, get away from the wall!"

Red shrugged, muttering, "Rub it in your chest." He did not like joining Boiler and Skinner in the sun. He led them to the road and stopped on the tormentor's edge of the guard's consciousness, turning to look up at Ledbetter. The guard had already disappeared back inside the air-conditioned tower. "Fickle," Red swore, reaching into his shirt pocket, separating a filtered cigarette from the crumpled pack. "We got a better view from here." He lit the cigarette, dragging deeply. Then he handed it to Boiler. "That's precious," he said, "go easy."

"Dude, damn man," Boiler nodded, eyeing the cigarette before dragging and handing it back to Red. "Everything that's cool is contraband. Five freaking bucks for a smoke!"

"If I paid for them," Red said.

"That's a hundred bucks a pack, dude. A grand a carton. You getting that much, Red?"

"You want any of this, Skinner?" Red asked. Skinner was half turned away, out of the path of the smoke. He shook his head. "No?" Red shrugged, returning his attention to Boiler. "The guards hit us up for four-hundred off the top. They got to get their piece of the action."

"Damn, dude," Boiler said, taking the proffered cigarette. "If you can't beat 'em bribe 'em. Man, it's easier to get cocaine in here than aspirin. Cigarettes ain't even illegal on the streets. Is that what Wheeler's mueling for you? He packing cigarettes?

"No," Red shook his head. "And don't hog that."

Boiler handed the butt to Red. Dragging deeply, Red handed it back.

"Keep it," he said.

"Yeah," Skinner said, snapping his fingers. "You're right, Red. The gates are like a picture. It's all perspective. You can't see a picture good if you are too close. He raised his arm and hand, pointing a long finger. "You see there," he said, cocking his head, seeming to study the sun lit gates. "The way the bars kind of wave in the sun and the walls frame them? Just like a picture. You got to get away from it to see it. Huh, Red?"

"That's smart," Boiler grunted. "Dude, you're real smart, pointing at the gates. Why don't you send 'em a message, tell 'em we're waiting for him?" He shook his head. "Give 'em our names while your at it! Tell them we're gonna kill the fat punk if he doesn't bring Red's shit! What the shit is wrong with you? What are you thinking? We were better off under the tower. At least there was shade. And that shit," he added, nodding at the gates, "that ain't no picture."

"Red said we could see better from here. Huh, Red? You don't know nothing, Boiler. Not about art. Nothing about it. I read about it in "Easy Rider."

"Dude, you can't read."

"I got a G.E.D."

"You better give it back. It ain't yours. Anyway, how come I got to read and write your letters, if you got a G.E.D.? Who took the test for you?"

Red, disgusted, had heard enough. "Hey, chill!"

"Screw him, Red," Skinner whined, staring hard at Boiler who had turned his back and was standing in the middle of the road. "I've got a G.E.D."

"Yeah, we all got G.E.D.'s, Red said. "We are all real fucking smart. That's why we're here."

Red did not doubt Skinner's claim. The G.E.D was like everything else in the joint. There were ways around everything. Skinner could have paid someone to take the test for him.

Boiler swung around, looking at Red. "You should have given me the shank," he said.

"What's that supposed to mean?" Skinner demanded. He stepped over in close to stand directly in front of Boiler. The shank was in Skinner's waistband, inside the jeans, the butt bulging against his shirt. The weapon had been made in the woodshop and was a steel, twelve-inch wood file, the rat-tail sharpened to a point, the blunt end wrapped in black electricians tape. When it was used, it would be dropped, left behind, the tape masking the fingerprints. Skinner's fingers hesitantly sought the handle, barely touching it through his shirt. "Fuck you," he warned Boiler, angrily pressing up as close to Boiler as he could get without actually touching him.

"No, fuck you!" Boiler growled. "Fuck you! You think you're gonna pull that on me? Then go on. Pull that shit. Take it out."

Skinner was supposed to be better than Boiler with a knife, which was why Red had given it to Skinner, but Red knew better than to take sides. "Fuck this," he said, looking up at the tower for Ledbetter. "What is this?" Without thinking, he found himself stepping between them, shoving them apart and turning from one to the other until he stopped and stood facing Skinner. "Fuck this!" he shouted at Skinner. "I'm telling you. Chill. Save this shit. You bring that Ledbetter down on us, I'll stick you myself. I'm not your bitch. Don't screw me. You want to kill each other, do it your own time. I'm telling you, knock it off. I'm telling you."

"Hey man," Skinner retreated, stepping back. "Hey, Red, I thought we were pals. I got a G.E.D., man."

"Forget that shit," Red told him. "Listen, both of you. You know what to do?"

"Yeah, Red," Skinner nodded.

"Yeah, dude," Boiler said. "If he ain't got your shit, I grab him and Skinner does him."

"No," Red shook his head. "No. You wait until I tell you. Listen. You-wait-until-I-tell-you. You got that? When I tell you, Boiler, you grab him. Then Skinner, you do him. You got that? You wait until I tell you."

"Yeah, Red," Skinner said. "You tell us, Red. Then we hit him."

Red nodded. "You wait for me to tell you."

"Yeah, Red," Skinner agreed. "What's Wheeler packing anyway? What is he bringing you, Red? All he does outside is cut grass at guards' houses."

Red's nerves were beginning to fray. He took a deep breath, looking up at the gun tower. He had once heard the when Skinner got friendly with you, the only chance you might have was to kill him quick. In Youth Authority, fifteen years old and serving time for car theft, Skinner, after an argument with his fourteen-year-old cellmate, he talked the kid into letting him tie him up, telling him, he would show him how to escape. Skinner had spent the night torturing him, cutting his throat the next morning. There had been two other killings on the yard that Red knew of, but however crazy Skinner might be, Red did not think he was foolish enough to go up against him. Besides, they were Bikers, Skinner would need the Bikers' permission to whack Red, and that was not going to happen, but it was something else to worry Red. He would have felt better if he could have spit, but his mouth was dry.

"Alright," he said, suddenly deciding Ledbetter's little act had been the guards way of letting him know he was in the tower. "Fuck it."

He pushed past Skinner and crossed the grass to stand with his back to the wall below the tower. Boiler and Skinner followed him and stood flanking him, so that Red had to lean forward, looking past Skinner to the gates.

Red was no strong-arm artist. He was a thief, and perhaps the best and worst he could say for himself was that he could not keep his hands off other peoples property; especially, big ticket items, which necessarily involved risk and were never worth it, and that was exactly what he told himself, finding himself busted, sitting in a holding tank or jail or courtroom. It wasn't worth it, and he was beginning to think the same thing about Wheeler. It was not simply Wheeler's vulnerability, Red's own personality and emotions were involved. For Red, the ex-judge's fall represented proof of the hypocrisy of a system whose teeth had forever been stuck in Red's throat, sucking away his life, stealing it with no more right to it than Red had to steal what belonged to others, and Red, even if he only felt it and had not put it into words, wanted compensation for what they had done to him. It was only fair. If he had to pay, then they had to pay, and Wheeler was the only "they" available.

Red had approached Wheeler on the upper yard, and had been willing to pay for what he wanted from Wheeler, but the fat man had been scared of Red, and had broken down, melting into a sniveling tub of sweating jelly. Red could smell the fear. Wheeler reeked of it, and Red's disgust and hatred for authority, never far beneath the surface, and contempt for Wheeler, had taken over. Wheeler would do what Red wanted, or Red would cut his fucking head off.

It was not until later, after Wheeler had tried to bluff his way past Red, that Red had decided people like Wheeler, people who once had money and power, who had betrayed their trust, and had been ruined and shamed by it, destroying themselves, either accepted it and shot themselves, or denied it and kept denying it, living a lie, unable to accept that their claws had been pulled and they were finished, and should shoot themselves.

Red had waited for Wheeler, as he was waiting now. The fat man had come through the gates, seen Red, and kept walking, attempting to hide and lose himself among the other trustees. Red had exploded. Running up behind Wheeler, he had grabbed the back of the fat man's collar and jerked him backwards off his feet, slamming him down on his back. Wheeler had deflated and in the orange coveralls had looked like flattened road kill.

"You stupid?" Red had shouted, pushing a finger into Wheeler's bloodless face. "Are you stupid?" he had repeated. "You know what happens to stupid people? Don't you?" Wheeler's head wagged, vigorously, his eyes closed, mouth open, working wordlessly. "Then you understand me?" Again, the head wagged. Red punched a finger hard into Wheeler's forehead, pushing at it and standing up. He tapped the toe of his boot against Wheeler's ribs. "You keep your eyes closed. Get used to it," he had said, leaving Wheeler quelled and trembling with one final word, "Monday," which was today.

But Wheeler was not the sole complication. The Bikers were Red's family; he had considered what was between him and Wheeler personal. He'd had no intentions of involving the Bikers, but word had gotten around after his set-to with Wheeler, so that Red had needed to go to the Bikers and explain what was happening. They had given him a hard time, and he'd had a few bad moments, suddenly wondering if Wheeler's "luck" at staying alive had anything to do with him paying protection to the Bikers and other gangs on the yard. Fear, as with any gang, was the Bikers' stock and trade. If Red meant to whack Wheeler, they wanted it known on the yard that it was a Biker hit. The ex-judge was a big fish. All Red had to do was give the word and walk away. He would be in the clear, except that they all knew it was not that easy. Five minutes afterwards every snitch in the joint would have a kite into the

Captain. Even if Boiler and Skinner kept their mouths shut, someone was certain to put Red at the scene, so that the best he could hope for was a year in administrative segregation. Not that it mattered. What mattered was that he was a Biker, and if he broke Biker law, there would be no second or third strike. They did not give passes and their response would be quick enough to make even the most bloodthirsty prosecutors green with envy. If Wheeler crossed Red now, and Red let it go, the Bikers would whack Boiler and Skinner, along with Red, for allowing Red to fail the Bikers.

"Hey, man," Skinner asked, "what do you think he'll say?"

"Wheeler?"

"Naw. Ledbetter."

"Ledbetter?" Red shrugged. "It's not my problem."

"He was sleeping," Boiler said.

"Maybe they'll fire him," Skinner said.

"No, dude," Boiler said. "They won't fire him. They'll give him a medal. They want Wheeler dead."

"Yeah?" Skinner perked up. "Why's that?"

"He's a symbol."

"What kind of symbol?"

"I don't know," Boiler said. "Because he snitched on them. You know, he let them down."

"That it, Red?" Skinner asked. "How'd he get to be a trustee anyway?"

"The bulls like having a big shot like him hanging around," Red explained. "You know, doing their gardening, hauling their trash, whatever. An ex-judge. He's where he belongs, on his knees in the dirt."

"Yeah," Skinner agreed. "What's he supposed to have anyway? What's he got you want, Red?"

"Red ain't telling you, dude. Why don't you leave it alone?"

"Chill," Red interrupted, cutting off Skinner before an argument started. "You guys remember when we hit Animal? Quick? Real quick? Quick."

Boiler shrugged. "Yeah, sure, you cut his throat."

"Doc and me. He grabbed him and I did him. He was dead and we were all gone before anyone knew what happened. Quick. Remember? All right? Quick."

The murmuring of the trustee's voices was beginning to fill the cul-de-sac. Behind the gates, a guard with a clipboard moved among the trustees, checking individual identification cards against his paper lists. Ironically, getting back into the prison was as hard as getting out. Time slowed. The tower's shadow climbed and stretched itself across the wall. Finally, the jolt of a chain pulley rattled to life, grating against the metal guides, the gates separating with the trustees rushing into the cul-de-sac, hurrying along the road to the lower yard.

Skinner stepped away from the wall, "There he is, Red. In the back."

"I see him."

Wheeler looked like a Halloween pumpkin with a red, balloon face. He took his time, separating from the others and not moving towards Red until the last possible moment, dragging himself along with short, hesitating steps.

"Boiler," Red said, "wait until I tell you."

Boiler grunted as Wheeler stopped in front of Red.

Red greeted the man with a threat: "You better have it."

"Red, I... "

Grabbing Wheeler with both fists by the front of his coveralls, Red jerked him onto his toes and danced him around, shoving his back hard against the wall. "Don't you know I'll kill you?"

"No, no! I got it. Honest, Red. Honest, Red! Man!"

Red let go of him. "All right," he said, leaning in close to Wheeler, so close that he could smell the sour mixing of his own breath with Wheeler's terror. "Let me have it."

Wheeler's stubby fingers fumbled with metal buttons at his bulging waist. He reached inside the open coveralls, but hesitated, leaving his hand hidden as he lifted frightened, brown, saucer-like eyes to look up at the gun tower.

Boiler eased around behind Wheeler, pushing him away from the wall. Red stepped back, making room for Wheeler to move, but shook his head, meaning Boiler should forget the hit.

Skinner had moved over and stood close beside Red, to the side and front of Wheeler. "Com'on," he ordered Wheeler. "Give it to Red."

Wheeler continued to hesitate. "Red, if they bust me, I'll lose my trustee status. I'll go to the hole. I could lose my parole date."

"You're breaking our hearts," Boiler said.

Red held out his hand, palm up, fingers crawling. "Let's see it."

"I had to risk it," Wheeler said, reluctantly

drawing his hand from inside the coveralls, showing Red the tiny white fur ball. "I almost didn't get it."

"I'll be damned!" Skinner exclaimed. "Son of a bitch!"

Yeah, you almost didn't get it," Red said sarcastically, taking it from Wheeler. It lay small in Red's big hand, light, like nothing, like the air, only soft. He touched its' spiny back, feeling the bones, the fur smoothing, brushing the end of his fingers. It moved its' pink nose against Red's palm. He saw its' eyes and seemed suddenly alarmed. "Hey, wait! Is this thing sick? It's got blue eyes!"

"They're born with blue eyes," Wheeler told him.

"Yeah?" Red looked up into the fat man's sweaty face. "Are you still here?"

Boiler, behind Wheeler, gave him a shove sideways towards the road. "Go on, dude," he told him. "Beat it."

"Yeah," Skinner said as the fat man hurried away. "Put an egg in your shoe and beat it."

"All this shit for a cat," Boiler said, not disguising his disgust. "We were gonna kill a dude for a cat?"

Red raised his head, looking at Boiler. "You don't like it?"

Boiler looked at the kitten. "No, it's not that, Red," he said. It's cool, dude."

"It's like a baby," Skinner said. "Hey, man. Sometimes we can help raise it. Can't we man? Me and Boiler, too? Sometimes we can baby-sit for you. Can't we Boiler?"

"You can't baby-sit no cat," Boiler said. "It ain't a baby,"

"Maybe its Red's baby," Skinner said. Did you think of that? Huh, Red? He has to take care of it. And we can baby-sit. We're Red's pals, ain't we? Can I carry it, Red? How about it?"

"No, I got it," Red said. It would not be easy, raising a kitten, keeping it away from the guards, but he had it now and would do what it took to keep it.

Paul Ferguson

SCHOKA

I was at San Quinton when George Jackson killed
four people – two guards and two inmates – and
cut up three others, leaving them for dead as he
and his partner, Spain broke out of the
Adjustment Center. It just so happened I came up
the stairs from the lower yard and was standing
under the gun bull that spotted Jackson running
down the ramp in the direction of the lower alley.
I heard the shot and saw him fall. Spain was
crouching in the bushes in front of the chapel.

Schoka

Schoka

Schoka was well under six-feet and was
thin. His color was a golden brown with a slick
shaved head, a long face with small, black, deep-
set eyes, a narrow nose, and perfectly white teeth.
He was dressed in white coveralls and chained
hands and feet and was followed by a lanky, red-
necked guard in a wrinkled khaki uniform as he
entered the long shadows of the administrations
building's foyer to hobble up the wooden stairs to
the landing, turning down a short, unlit hall into a
huge, dimly lit room used for visiting attorneys.

The glass of the many tall windows across
the front of the room was painted with a streaky
dark green and the dozen wooden conference
tables and straight back chairs along side of the
tables were empty, except for the pretty redhead
sitting with a burnished leather briefcase on her
lap at a table midway across the room, waiting for
Schoka.

The guard stopped Schoka with a word
and visually rechecked the handcuffs before telling
him to "go ahead and join the lady." Schoka hated
the guard because he was a guard or maybe
because he was white. Schoka did not really need a
reason since it came back to him being black and a
prisoner, always knowing if he needed a reason, he
could choose from four-hundred years of reasons

192

Paul Ferguson

with nothing ever changing. Slavery for blacks in
the United States hadn't gone away, but had
evolved, persevering, becoming more savvy with
its home in the ever expanding industrial prison
complex, vampiric, its savage teeth in the throats
of the black and poor, living on their blood, so
that if anything had changed, he couldn't tell. He
was still a slave and the devils eating him alive
were still white. Believing the lanky redneck
wouldn't react in front of the woman, Schoka
pointedly turned rudely close into him, forcing the
surprised guard to step back out of Schoka's way
as he started across the hardwood floor in jerking
steps, the restraining cuffs on his ankles, the
miffed guard slowly moving over to sit down
behind the desk beside the open door to the hall.

   The waiting woman was Helen Mare. She
was rich, and though Schoka didn't know why she
worked, since she was rich, she was an attorney
partnered with a law firm in San Francisco. The
court had appointed her to file an appeal on his
thirty-year sentence for dealing drugs. She
evidently was good at her job and was a straight
shooter. Five minutes after she'd first had him
brought to the interviewing room and had
introduced herself, sitting down with him, she'd
told him not to get his hopes up, and there wasn't
much anyone could do for him. He'd already
know that much, but there was something else
going on with her. She was looking hard, tossing
her head and blinking to keep from staring at him.
There was no telling about women, black or white,
but he'd recognized the look and since one way or
another he'd destroyed every other connection
he'd had with anyone outside the walls, he'd
decided to follow his instincts. Now, after almost

a year of making love to her across the table and through the mails, she was the key to his escape plan.

Unless she had betrayed him, there was a gun in the briefcase she held in her lap.

She smiled nervously as he sat down opposite her. She had been drinking. Her blue eyes were shiny and wider than usual. The pinpoint black irises darted away from his look to the pale green walls and high, white ceiling. He sniffed through the pervading fragrance of Xeryus, catching the faint hint of Johnnie's Black Label and mint. His brown face reddened as he clamped his mouth shut, staring at her in disbelief.

She was no empty headed kid and knew the consequences for them both if she was caught smuggling him the gun. Although she wasn't nearly drunk, she was stupidly risking everything. The contents of the briefcase were legally privileged and couldn't be searched when she entered the prison without probable cause or a court order. The smell of scotch on her breath could have provided the guards with probable cause. They had either missed it or ignored it, and she'd walked the gun in the briefcase past them. She'd done it, but he couldn't help comparing her to whores he'd known. They'd also had the looks and pretty clothes, showing themselves and their wares off, but no matter how smart they were, they had lacked common sense and had needed to be watched and told what to do every moment. And it wasn't just the gun worrying him. When she left him, she had to go to the airport. She had a plane to catch. His plan called for her to be safely away before her part in the escape was discovered. He'd arranged for a forged passport and she was to leave money and a ticket to South America for him to pick up. He would join her at the Ambassador in Rio next week. She needed a clear head and that meant laying off the booze.

"No more of that," he said.

"Oh come on," she shot back, impatiently. "It was only one at lunch. I had to do something while waiting to get in here."

"No more."

"Hello," she said. "I'm here. Shouldn't that count? And I have it. You want to see?"

He leaned forward to the table, nodding, and she lifted the boxy briefcase, set it between them in from of her, and opened it, the snap catches springing up with echoing metallic clicks. Her slender, well-manicured fingers, hidden from his view by the back of the open case, quickly found the gun among the legal papers. He saw it glimmer, vaguely reflected in her eyes, as she cautiously picked it up. Covering it with her free hand, she moved it from the case, down over the table's edge and then, leaning low, held the gun out at arm's length under the table, waiting for him to take it from her.

The irritation in his black eyes shifted to a blinking, wordless concern about the attention of the guard at the desk some fifteen feet directly behind him. He didn't know if she was being reckless, made brave by the booze. In fact, he really knew little about her, having spent all his time with her confined to this room at this very table. She always sat in the same place, entering the room through the electronically controlled dark green steel door that opened in the corner onto an outer waiting room and was diagonally convenient to the table. Her moods were always questionable and she could be cold and distantly professional or warm and girl sweetish, or up and down on the scale anywhere, changing from one persona or another without notice. He didn't know what to expect and didn't know how it felt to hold or kiss her, having her naked in his arms. He'd seldom been able to touch her, even her hand. He wanted her terribly, but didn't love her. Although at time, the pain in his loins cramping unbearably, he had to remind himself he was using her and wasn't escaping to be with her, but to reclaim his life. He often suspected she might be and alcoholic or worse, like some crazy, rich white bitches he'd heard of who sought out black men, determined to ruin everyone's life, doing penance for the sins of their fathers, and she was an attorney and him a black convict, so maybe that was an added guilty attraction, but these were twisting labyrinths beyond his ability. He couldn't figure what she expected of him, beyond obviously wanting a real man, something he suspected must be rare in her world, but he didn't know what else she wanted, or what else there was. And, too, he would have been more settled within himself if he could have placed her in some time period, but even this was denied him. She refused to tell her age. He thought her somewhere in her early-thirties, but she had herself all together and was beautiful, and like all beauty it was pointless and blinding, so that following it led nowhere and was deceptive with her makeup and luxurious red hair done just so, framing her bright, finely chiseled features, and she was a sharp dresser, youthfully clothing her svelte, well tuned body with the latest by Armani or Gucci, or the sexy stuff by Valentino, demonstrating a prejudice for satin and cashmere and Bill Blass sable jackets. She seemed to love jangling, designer jewelry, but she'd told him of student protests at Berkley and the People's Park as if she'd been present, and at twenty-five he barely remembered hearing of them, though he'd been raised in Black Panther country in Oakland. She'd also been married, at least twice, maybe three or four times, and was divorced. She maybe was in her forty's and it was her money that made the difference.

Of course, money always made the difference. He knew that and was quick enough about most things and was street smart, but in many ways was naive. He'd grown up in a thorny briar patch, in a dark ruins bombed dumb by poverty and caught in a crossfire of black violence and problems that didn't even exist in the white, moneyed world. She knew nothing about that, except in a sad, abstract way, and he'd only found out what his life had really been like after he'd started dealing and river of cash had flowed through his two-toned hands, introducing him to a whole new life. A life he was only beginning to appreciate when the cops came busting in and the law had taken it, along with everything else he owned, including the rest of his life. One thing he did know, it was money that mattered and it was money he would need when he was back on the streets. She had it and without her the escape wouldn't be possible.

He smiled, hopefully, reassuringly, showing his pearly whites, trusting her to warn him if the guard moved from the desk as he dropped his cuffed wrists into his lap, reaching under the table. His fingers met her sharp, pink claws and the soft, damp flesh of her fingers and hands. Finding the hard, unseen metal, he took it between his own pink palms and pulled his hands from under the table. With a quick look down he saw a pearl handled, chrome plated, five-inch .32 automatic with five shots in the clip; a woman's gun. Her gun. Although short on killing power, it would have to do. He shoved it quickly out of sight inside the elastic waistband of his coveralls. His stomach tightened, retreating from the cruel touch of the deadly metal, but he swelled with pride in himself. He might not know her, but scared as she was, he had control over her, and nothing else mattered. He continued smiling, watching as, with a business-like air, she closed the briefcase, snapping the locks shut and moving the case off the table to stand it on the floor beside her chair.

"You're dangerous, girl," he said, "Man," winking admiringly as he spoke, "You know I love you."

Her face saddened. Now tears began in her eyes.

She was going to make leaving him harder than it had to be. "Girl, no. Don't do that."

She nodded. "I'm sorry," she said, lifting her head up and back to contain the tears. Wiping her eyes, her fingers were careful to avoid smearing the eyeliner. "It's just – I wish there was another way. There isn't, is there?"

She looked into his face, her eyes shining with a distillation of tears and alcohol. They both knew it was too late. "I love you," he said, feeling the gun against his stomach. He knew smuggling the gun had pushed her limits, with her every instinct against what she was doing, and she had to be out of it and taking it hard, so that it might not take a lot to turn her back. He had to keep her dreaming and from falling apart and that meant assuring her she wasn't in over her head. "You don't have to worry. I won't hurt anyone. I'm going to round up the guards and keep them quiet. It's all right."

"I know."

"Do you have to go?"

She raised her arm, turning her wrist to look at the diamond watch face of the gold bracelet. "I won't miss my flight."

"There's no time, man," he said. The procedure was for him to remain seated while she got up from the table and left the room. He could then get up to be escorted out of the building and across the big yard to the cell house, in his case, the punishment block. He intended to escape from there where friends were waiting to help him, but she made no effort to stand and leaned toward the table, looking at him with her arms folded across her breasts. "It's all right," he said. "You'll see. It's like I planned. Nothing to it, man. Com'on girl, smile for me, man. You can't miss your plane.

"I can't… I can't believe in anything."

"Me, mon," he said. "I'm your prince. You believe in me, girl." He laughed. "Just you think, now, mon, you'll be in Rio tonight!" He lowered his voice. "And I'll be there next week."

"I'll be alone!" she said fiercely and too loud.

He hushed her, motioning. "It won't be for long. I'll be there, man. You wait for me. I'll be there!"

II

After the bright sun of the dusty big yard, the crepuscular gloom inside the punishment block blinded Schoka but he knew the drill and could see well enough. His vision slowly clearing, he stopped in front of the long, narrow sally-port of bars, like a lion's cage, with a gate at either end. The lanky redneck, key in hand, stepping close, removed the chains and cuffs from Schoka's wrists and bent down in front of the black prisoner to unlock the ankle cuffs, Schoka, lifting one foot and then the other, aiding the guard's efforts. Schoka envisioned himself kicking the stooping redneck in the face while whipping the gun out from inside his coveralls, throwing down on the guard, but he knew it would be a mistake. No matter how good it would feel to see fear in the redneck's eyes, it would be stupid and premature. Schoka couldn't afford to indulge his hatred or let it get in the way. It was just personal and the redneck had never actually done anything toward him. Revenge wasn't worth blowing the escape, so, with the cuffs off, he entered the shadowy cage, not waiting to be told. The guard banged the gate behind Schoka, shaking it, checking the lock, and then, the cuffs and chains loosely hanging in one hand, the radio at his belt squawking with a sudden burst of static, he turned away and went back out the iron door onto the big yard, leaving Schoka to be released from the sally-port by the punishment block officer.

Schoka walked to the front of the cage. A low roar like the echo of a gigantic spiral shell infused the tenebrous shadows, but he barely noted the sound or the souring smells that impregnated the massive building. He'd lived with the dark and noise and smells for over eighteen months and was immune to them and suspected he could get used to about anything. The punishment block was the oldest building in the prison and was over a hundred and fifty years old and was a foul, dirty place filled with the seemingly endless four by seven tombs of the living dead. During the day, a half-light came from the glowing gray haze penetrating the filthy glass of the rolls of tall, arched windows high up along the interior sidewalls and every kind of vermin occupied the shadows. At night, when sparsely spaced low wattage bulbs barely lit the tiers, casting yellow shadows into a few lucky cells, allowing inmates with books to read or stationary to write letters, rats as big as house cats could be heard squealing and scurrying on the gallery while the black walls, if stared at, seemed to be alive, seething with masses of moving insects. A narrow bunk and toilet stool and cold-water sink occupied the otherwise bare cells and there was no hot water. Cold showers were given once a week, one tier at a time. Sixty naked inmates were released from their cells with the guards herding them down the stairs in a line to the back of the punishment block where for five shivering minutes they were forced to stand under one of fifteen drizzling showerheads, ordered to wash themselves with the freezing water. Morning and night a brown bag meal, consisting of two sandwiches, either of peanut butter or of cheese, and an orange or apple, with a waxed container of milk or grape punch, was pushed through the cell bars by a guard. Otherwise, with the exception of the showers and guards constant yelling between cells and the screaming howls that often erupted in pointless appeals for attention, there was little or no contact between inmates or with anyone else within the punishment block. Isolation within the system was the bottom line in America's prisons that we're all alike and the same; however old or new, computerized or not, the machinery was the same inside or on the streets. It was geared to handle anyone who failed to recognize that society, with its public opinions and God and cops, maintained itself by pure force, employing every extreme – from subtle exhortations to chains and death – deluding the naïve by hiding the untenable reality and always justifying the means, by the end. Ordinary people weren't born black or poor and didn't know what was being done in their names, and when they did know, didn't care because they didn't believe it could happen to them. Schoka envied them their ignorance and ability to deceive themselves and would have been content to be a fool's fool, except they had failed him and hadn't been able to keep his eyes closed. On opening them, he'd seen the master's iron hand everywhere and in everything, and though he'd learned to be a user, he remained a victim, conscious of himself in a life without hope. There was nothing he could change and it was too late to change himself with no way to forget. He couldn't forgive them and would not excuse them for failing him. Above all, he knew he wasn't wrong, putting his needs and desires first. Whatever he did, no matter how horrible or who suffered, he was what they had made of him and he could never even the score. The gun wouldn't give him a new life, but offered him a fresh start, and feeling it at his waist, his fingers pressing it against his stomach, reassured him. One way or another he was finished with them pushing him around. If he didn't escape, the guards wouldn't take him alive. He'd already decided not to quit or give up. He would rather be dead and have death for his purpose than to be buried alive for thirty years with no purpose.

He stopped at the front gate and stood looking through the bars. He saw a gray, red-faced guard sitting at a desk maybe twenty-feet away across the cement floor. The desk was between two rusty colored steel stairways that faced one another and were bolted to the end wall of the cellblock. The stairs climbed, zigzagging, up five flights to the tiers and cells stacked back-to-back, one on top of the other, the height and length of both sides of the cellblock. The old man at the desk between the stairs was leaning forward in his chair, reading a paperback book he held with one hand under the light of a desk lamp. Schoka didn't know him and had never seen him before, but knew no guard was ever in a hurry to disturb himself for an inmate and Schoka leaned with his back against the bars at the side of the cage, waiting for the old man.

Prison rules required inmates to be strip-searched before being returned to their cells. Schoka had to act before he was searched and the gun found. When the old man unlocked the sally-port, Schoka would have to quickly take him prisoner and keep him quiet, allowing him no opportunity to use his radio or alert the gun bulls patrolling the catwalks that ran in front of the windows along both side walks of the building. There were at least two other guards with radios on the tiers, patrolling the cellblock, but like the old man, they weren't armed and could easily be dealt with. The gun bulls, armed to the teeth with pistols and Winchesters, were another matter, and it would mean a quick end for Schoka himself if they discovered what was happening before he was ready to deal with them.

The catwalks and windows were essential to his plans. The prison was built on a peninsula and was surrounded by forty-foot sandstone walls, except for the punishment block. The walls stopped up against the sides of the massive, stone building, so its east sidewall windows looked out on a bay full of boats with nothing between Schoka and them, except the barred windows. He figured he and his 'home-boys' could jump across the eight feet separating the fourth tier from the east catwalk and tie sheets to the bars, twisting the sheets until the bars spread or pulled out of the wall. They could then climb down outside and steal a boat, or if necessary, it wasn't more than a mile across the shallow bay, swim to the woods on the far shore, hide until they could steal a car, then they were home free.

The key was taking the guards prisoner, locking them up and leaving just at dark before the alarm was given. The whole thing, with any luck, shouldn't take more than an hour, with another hour in the water. It sounded tricky and was dangerous, but could be done. The guards were mostly white and weren't heroes and were already scared of the blacks. Especially blacks in the punishment block.

He planned to use the guards fear and hoped to intimidate them, beginning with the old man at the desk, taking away his radio and waving the gun in his face, but Schoka had killed before, on the streets with a gun and twice on the big yard with a knife. He was prepared to kill again, but hadn't lied to Helen Mare. He didn't plan to kill anyone. He believed the earlier killings were necessary and didn't count. There'd been no problem, just something he'd had to do. Afterwards, he hadn't felt any different or been bothered by thinking about them and had known it was them or him and with nothing to keep it from being him except that he'd gotten to them first. Of course, this was now different. His earlier victims were black and he hadn't hated them. At the time, they were just business, old scores on the streets or from the streets that had caught up with him and he'd had to settle, but his primitive instincts were strong and existed along side his more rational self. The thought of having the guards at his mercy set his heart pounding and started his blood pulsing like fire through his veins, flushing his golden skin a darker red, exciting him with a flux of anticipation, which was almost sexual in nature. He was, after all, only human. Maybe he would take a little revenge, putting the fear of him into the guards, knocking their heads together if he got the chance. The gun made Schoka the man, but he didn't want to waste his few precious bullets. If it came to killing them, it would be better, quieter, if he had a knife. He actually preferred the meat-carving feel of a knife, the close contact with the kill. Getting blood on his hands somehow seemed to wash away the abuse he'd suffered.

His friends in their cells were waiting for him to release them. Maybe they would have a knife, although most of them depended on Schoka to lead them, telling them what to do.

The old man's chair scraped the floor as he slowly rose and came around the desk, the heavy, brass key to the sally-port gate in his fleshy, pale hand. Schoka looked for the old man's radio, saw he didn't have it, and then spotted it in its black case left carelessly sitting on the desk. Schoka couldn't have asked for anything more but that luck was with him. The old man was carelessly friendly and smiling with rubbery lips as he stopped in front of the gate.

"I know," he said, his smile widening to show yellowed teeth. "You think I'm slower than Christmas."

Up close, he was heavier than he looked

behind the desk and was wearing wire-framed glasses, the lenses magnifying his rheumy blue eyes. A black and white plastic nametag above the left shirt pocket identified him as "Officer Novak." He inserted the key; turning it, the lock clanging open.

Schoka threw his weight against the bars, slamming the gate into Novak, knocking him back and down to sprawl on the concrete floor. Schoka, gun in hand followed Novak, standing over him.

"Get up," Schoka growled in a hoarse whisper, waving the gun. "You want to die? Get up!"

Shaken, a bewildered look on his now white face, Novak automatically sat up, his hand trembling as he straightened his glasses. He stared up at Schoka.

"Give me that," Novak ordered, apparently unable to grasp the situation. "Where'd you get that?"

Schoka kicked him hard in the hip and a second time lower down in the thigh. "Get up! You want to die? Get up!"

Novak brought his arms up in front of his face. "Don't," he said with a dry cough. "I can't get up."

"I'll pop a cap in your ass!"

His face a painful grimace, Novak twisted

around, over onto his hands and knees and pushed himself unaided to his feet.

Schoka jammed the automatic into the folded fat of the old man's throat. Pushing up, lifting Novak to his toes, Schoka hissed, "I'll leave you right here!"

"Don't do it," Novak begged in a whisper. "I ain't done nothing to you people. What do you want?"

Schoka grabbed Novak by the back of his collar and jerked him around to the side in a half circle. A dozen isolation cells with rusted, solid iron doors made up the front bar of the first tier on the gallery. Schoka pushed the old man past the stairs and around the corner to the east side of the cellblock. The brass key was a master key, fitting the cell locks. Schoka opened the end cell. Finding it empty, he shoved Novak inside. As Schoka closed the door, he warned Novak, "Don't run your jaws, old man. Don't make me come back here."

Locking the door, Schoka turned and went back around to the front of the cellblock. He started up the metal stairs, taking them two at a time, the key in one hand, the gun in the other. He had men to release from their cells on the third and fourth tiers but first he had to find the other two guards. They made it easy for him and were standing together, talking on the third tier landing at the top of the stairs – the blonde Nazi bastard, Ziegler, and another skinny redneck, Brinks.

They must have heard him coming. They

had turned, looking over the stair rail. Their mouths dropped open as he raised the gun, pointing it at them and moving quickly up the stairs to the landing.

"Don't move," Schoka, winded, panted. "I'll waste you!" He was sweating and breathing hard, but was calm and in control. "I'll send your Nazi asses to Valhalla."

"That's Norse," Ziegler sneered.

Schoka lifted the gun, bringing the butt down hard across Ziegler's nose. The blonde jerked his head back. Grunting and covering his nose with both hands, he staggered against the wall. "God damn you!" he swore. Blood dripping down his wrists to the cuffs of his shirt and then to the floor in dark, red drops. "It's broke. You broke my goddamn nose!"

Schoka ignored him. "Give me the radios," he told Brinks. "Both of them. Put 'em on the floor."

"What're ya gonna do?" Brinks asked, unhooking his own and Ziegler's radio from their belts and setting them down between him and Ziegler. "You can't get out of here."

"Now the mace," Schoka told him. "On the floor."

Brinks sat the canisters of pepper spray down beside the radios. "Why don't you think, man?"

"Shut up. We're gonna let Clayton out. Now go on in front of me."

Brinks turned to start down the tier, but Ziegler hesitated. He was holding his bloody nose with one hand, looking over it, giving Schoka an icy stare.

"Do it, man," Schoka threatened. "I'll kill both of you or which one I can. Don't play me, man. You'll get Brinks killed. I ain't playing with y'all."

Brinks grabbed Ziegler' arm. "Come on," he said, pulling the arm. "We better do it."

The tier walks above overhung the tier walks below and Schoka counted on the fourth tier's walk to screen him and the guards on the third tier from the gun bull on the catwalk that was above them, opposite the fourth tier. The tier was full of shadows, but in any case, he wasn't really worried about being seen as he followed the guards along the tier rail. Clayton's cell was only a third of the way down the tier and Schoka knew from long hours of lying in his cell, observing the bulls during their different shifts, they mostly spent their time sitting at the far end of the catwalk at the back of the building, a distance of nearly three-hundred feet. The inmates in their cells were more of a problem. Black and white faces began appearing, pressed against the bars, entreating, as if they knew what was happening, their hands reaching out to touch Schoka.

"Schoka!"

"Let me out, brother!"

"Hey, man. Hey!"

"Schoka!"

"Take me, Schoka!"

"Schoka!"

"Chill, man," he repeated again and again. "Cool it. I'll be back," he lied. They were putting him on the spot, turning up the heat. He felt like he was running a gauntlet, the too loud voices like blows capable of attracting the gun bulls' attention. If a bull had been walking the east catwalk, looking down along the tiers, Schoka would have been busted, but there wasn't. He stopped Ziegler and Brinks in front of Clayton's cell.

Clayton was already pressed against the bars. "Whoa, shit, man!" he exclaimed. "That's a gun, baby! Damn, Schoka!"

"No, brother," Schoka said, unlocking and pulling open the cell door. "It's a boat, man. We're gonna sail right outta here."

Clayton was wearing a t-shirt, his heavily muscled shoulders and arms rippled as he stood in the open door. He smiled, poking Ziegler with a finger in the chest. "What about him?" he asked, ignoring Brinks.

"Let 'em in the cell."

"Go on," Clayton growled, stepping aside, out of the way. "Get in there!"

"We're getting outta here," Schoka said, pushing Ziegler into the cell and into Brinks' back, so that both guards stumbled.

"We gonna waste 'em, Schoka?" Clayton asked, staring past Schoka to the guards. "Waste 'em now!"

"No," Schoka shook his head. "No, we can't risk it."

"Cut 'em, brother. They mace me! Ziegler! Cut his white-ass, honky throat!"

Schoka pushed the cell door closed, turning the spike in the lock. "One sound," he promised, staring hard at Ziegler, "and Clayton comes back with the key."

"Fuck that," Clayton said. "Ain't we gonna at least tie 'em up? Do 'em, man!"

"No, man. We gotta get T.J. and Little Man and take out the gun bulls. We ain't got time for that shit."

"We gonna take the whole joint?"

"We're getting' outta here. Com'on."

He hurried Clayton back up the tier and quickly up the stairs to the fourth tier, stopping on the landing. Leaving Clayton behind him, standing against the wall, Schoka crossed to the side rail and cautiously leaned out. The automatic timer hadn't switched the tier lights on yet and the air was grainy with swaddling shadows. The glow had faded from the tall, arched windows along the wall and the long, narrow gap between the catwalk and tier was a dark chasm. A dim yellow bulb glowed above the door at the far end of the catwalk and by its light Schoka recognized the bull, a heavy set, young white guy – Candy. He had the wooden chair tipped up onto its back legs and was laying back in it, his head resting against the wall. His rifle was a thin, black stick across his fat lap, and unless he had suddenly changed his ways, he would be wearing headphones, which meant he probably had his headphones plugged into a walkman and his eyes were closed, listening to the music, oblivious to whatever was happening around him. Schoka knew Candy wasn't the exception to the rule. Mostly the gun bulls would have been useless in real jobs and weren't much good as correctional officers. When they weren't reading or listening to walkmans, they were sleeping and were seldom seen actually moving along the catwalks, but Schoka couldn't afford to get careless. The far end of the tier was right in front of Candy and he could easily see the rest of the tier by standing up and turning his head. To reach T.J. and Little Man's cells, which were midway between him and Candy, Schoka would need to keep low and close to the cells and away from the rails. If Candy spotted Schoka, it would mean a running gunfight with Candy as well as whomever the bull was on the west catwalk. At any distance, the .32 automatic would be like spitting beans at the bulls with about the same effect. On the other hand, Candy might hesitate to get close enough to bluff into surrendering, which was Schoka's original intent. Although now, with the tension mounting in him and time short, he would need to improvise. The automatic wouldn't make much noise, and if he could release his friends, leading them back to Clayton, he could leave them and go up to the fifth tier, above Candy, and by staying low, get close enough to shoot him. Schoka could then jump across to the catwalk and with Candy's weapons, take on the other gun bull. The sight of Schoka with a gun would probably startle Candy into surrendering, but there was no time to waste. It would just be quicker to shoot.

Whatever Schoka meant to do, he had to do it quickly. The normal roar from the cells had already increased abnormally with his name being constantly whispered, passed from cell to cell, the refrain, "Schoka! Schoka!" was emerging dominating the roaring echoes.

"You hear that?" Clayton asked.

Schoka nodded, frowning. "They want out," he said. "Look, you stay here, man. I'll get T.J. and Little Man and come back."

Schoka, bending low, ducked around the corner onto the tier. He sped past the cells, ignoring their occupants, offering them no opportunity to interfere with him. On reaching the waiting T.J.'s cell, Schoka unlocked the door and opened it barely wide enough for the slender T.J. to wriggle out onto the tier.

T.J. squatted down beside Schoka.

"Man—" T.J. started, but Schoka cut him off, whispering, "Chill, man. Go on, Clayton's on the landing. I'll get Little Man."

T.J. nodded and started down the tier. Schoka duck-walked past another three cells, stopping in a squat in front of Little Man's cell. Little Man was ready and smart enough to keep his mouth shut. He wasn't much to look at and like his name, he was a little man, not much over five-feet tall and was thin and black as a stick, with long, braided hair, also like sticks, framing a narrow, bony face; but he was a country boy, and once they reached the woods, Little Man would be worth his weight in gold. He eagerly watched as Schoka inserted the key, turning it softly in the lock and opening the door only wide enough to allow Little Man to squeeze out onto the tier.

Schoka pointed with Little Man nodding and starting down the tier, followed by Schoka. The building was almost completely dark now and Schoka expected the lights on the tier overhang to switch on at any time. His prospects for taking out Candy were better in the dark. Everything seemed to be taking a long time and he felt tired, though it had gone, more or less, like he'd planned and there was no reason for him to be tired. He was in control and thinking clearly – maybe too clearly since he couldn't see how it would end.

Clayton and T.J. were waiting for him. Schoka squashed the reunion celebration by ignoring the smiles and outreached hands. He squatted down with his back against the wall, signaling them to join him. They gathered around him in a crescent moon, their eyes intent on his face, their heads almost touching.

"We got to jam," he said. "I'll go upstairs and take out Candy from the end of the tier. You all hang until you see him fall. Then cross to the catwalk. I'll get the other bull. We'll need sheets to spread the bars and something to stick between the sheets, so we can twist them up tight. It's almost dark –"

"What the hell is going on here?"

Schoka jerked his head up and saw Ricks standing on the west catwalk, looking across the landing at him. Ricks had his rifle, but wasn't pointing it, rather was holding it at rest, in the crook of his left arm. Without knowing what he meant to do, Schoka stood up and walked toward Ricks. When Schoka reached the rail, with no more than eight or ten feet separating him from Ricks, Schoka raised his arm and stabbed the air with the automatic, pulling the trigger. It was as if he threw the bullet out of the gun and it was an awkward gesture and seemed infinitely young and like a child playing cowboys and Indians, so that it wouldn't have surprised anyone if Schoka had shouted "Bang," or "You're dead!" or something else as naively instructive or insistent. There was an eternity in there with time slowing before the gun popped and popped again. Ricks slumped back, dropped the rifle, and then stumbled forward, tumbling over the rail, his body twisting in air as it fell through the reverberating echoes to the cement floor four stories below. Then the moments caught up like a car driving through a brick wall with Schoka spinning around, running across the landing to see Candy on his feet while almost at the same moment the catwalk entrance behind Candy opened. The bright light in the stairwell outside the door silhouetted the first and then a second gun bull. The second bull carried what looked like a sub-machine gun and was a Thompson. He immediately brought it up to his hip and stood spraying the fourth tier walk. The echoing rattle of the explosions and ricochets were thunderous, but only a little louder than the terrified screams issuing from the cells.

Schoka ducked down behind the wall. The others were on the floor, on their stomachs, with their hands up, covering their heads. Schoka was having trouble breathing and could hear his pulse pounding in his ears. He didn't know what had gone wrong, unless, maybe the old man had been discovered missing. It didn't really matter. Ricks was dead, and if they caught Schoka, he would spend every day of what was left of his life, at least until they executed him, in a strip cell. He had nothing to lose and wouldn't be taken alive.

All this time he had been holding the brass key. He unwrapped his fingers, letting it fall, the key ringing against the concrete floor. He pushed himself off the wall and went around Clayton to the stairs and down the steps to the third tier. The tier's overhang protected him from the pounding it was taking from the Thompson. He stayed away from the rail, close against the cell bars. Inmates in several cells along the tier had the cotton mattresses and blankets pulled off the beds and were hiding under the mattresses or behind them, holding them up between themselves and the front of their cells. A second Thompson was firing on the west side of the building. He hadn't heard the gas bombs, but knew they would get around to them soon or later. He was afraid, worried about being seen from the catwalk and not getting to Ziegler and Brinks. They belonged to him and were all he had left and he didn't want to leave them behind.

He reached their cell and shoved the automatic through the bars. The bed's mattress was lumped up on the floor, wedged in the narrow space between the bed's metal legs and the wall. The guards were standing on it. They backed away from the gun with Brinks behind Ziegler, until Brinks reached the toilet and couldn't back any further. He grabbed Ziegler and tried to hold the blonde in front of him. Ziegler jerked away. Stumbling over the mattress, he sat down hard on the edge of the bedsprings. The blood, smeared across his nose and cheeks, had dried black against his pale face and was black down his shirtfront. He was sweating heavily, but his eyes were hard and full of hate and his jaw was set. Schoka knew the look, having worn it often enough himself. Whatever the question, the answer was blood.

"Fuck you," Ziegler said.

Schoka shot him in the throat almost without realizing he had pulled the trigger. The bullet must have hit a jugular. It was like Ziegler's neck had sprung a leak with the blood spraying out. Ziegler grabbed his throat, pressing the wound hard, but couldn't stop the blood from running out under his hand. He jumped up, howling and wildly threw himself against the bars, trying to reach Schoka. Schoka stepped back startled, but knew Ziegler couldn't reach him.

Ziegler must also have known, but was ferocious and crazy mad. He backed up on the mattress and again launched himself into the bars, bouncing off them. He kept at it until he finally stumbled back exhausted. His legs buckled and he went down in a heap on the mattress, his shoulders propping him up against the bed frame. He must have known he was finished. He let go of his throat, the blood pulsing out in slow spurts. Without looking at Schoka, Ziegler lifted his bloody hand up, the index finger extended.

Brinks was moaning, big eyed. His hair and khaki's were wet with perspiration. He was bent down in front of the sink, pulling at the mattress, but couldn't move Ziegler's weight enough to lift the mattress up to protect himself. Schoka almost felt sorry for Brinks' desperate struggle. There was nowhere to hide. Schoka aimed carefully and pulled the trigger. The sound of the automatic was lost in the echoing thunder of the Thompson's. A tiny black dot appeared in Brinks' forehead above his right eye. He collapsed backwards to lay dead under the sink beside the toilet.

Schoka turned and ran back up the tier and up the stairs. The noise of the Thompson's had decreased to sporadic rat-tat-tat bursts, ricochets careened off the walls, breaking out the windows. The cowered prisoners in their cells had settled into silence. Little Man was alone on the landing. He was kneeling, holding his face in his hands with his back against the wall.

Schoka went to him. "What happened? Where are T.J. and Clayton?"

Little Man moaned, making no other answer. His body shook, trembling with fear. Schoka put his hands on Little Man's shoulder, shaking him.

"Talk to me!"

Little Man kept his face covered, mumbling through his hands. "They gone, Schoka."

"Gone? Gone where?"

"They lookin' for you,"

They were probably dead, the cause of the Thompson firing on the far side of the building. He hoped they were dead.

"I got Ziegler."

"Why you killed them mens?" Little Man moaned. "They gonna kill us now for sure." He dropped his hands; his red eyes were wide and shiny with tears. "What my momma gonna say, Schoka? We gotta pray, brother. Schoka you pray."

Schoka rubbed Little Man's bony shoulder. "We'll pray," he said.

The automatic had one precious bullet left. He had not wanted to sacrifice it on the old guard downstairs. He was keeping it for himself. He saw he had to help Little Man.

"You pray," he told Little Man.

"I know the Our Father," Little Man said. He closed his eyes, bowing his head. "Our Father who are in Heaven –"

Schoka raised the automatic, holding it close to the side of Little Man's head, almost touching the cornrows. The Thompson's had stopped their rattling. The sound of the automatic echoed to come back muffled and far away. The Thompson's began firing. Little Man's hair was on fire. It flared and went out as he seemed to relax into himself, slumping back on his heels to slide down the wall. Schoka laid him down. It was all he could do. Schoka didn't know if there was a God, but hoped there was a green pasture somewhere for Little Man.

The Thompson's continued to fire. Schoka stood and walked to the corner of the wall. He ripped open the white coveralls, exposing his black chest and stepped around the corner and into the open. Candy was on the catwalk not twenty feet away. Schoka saw Candy turn, holding the rifle in front of him as he ran down the catwalk away from Schoka to the guard with the Thompson. Schoka thought it too bad the automatic was empty. He could have shot Candy in the back.

"Hey you mother fuckers, shoot me!"

He raised the automatic, pointing it at arms length at the gun bull with the Thompson. Schoka saw the bull turn and immediately felt the bullets burn through his chest. The force swung

Schoka around, bouncing him off the wall, but somehow he stayed on his feet and started back around the corner to Little Man.

Dying was like Schoka had always heard. Things were getting dark, far away, and then close, big, and then far away. It was not so bad, although he would never see Rio. He hoped Helen had listened to him and was safe. A kind of anguish filled him. He did not want to think about her. He was shrinking, or at least, the floor was getting closer. The pain inside him burned and was huge and unbelievable, as if the building was sitting on his chest.

He found he was lying on the floor and tried to push himself back up. He could not move his arms. He could feel them, they were okay, but he could not move them. He laid still, his eyes closed, blood spreading around him in ever widening circles.

Paul Ferguson

GAVOTTE

The word derives from the Middle-French,
Gavato, meaning Mountain Dweller. Barbara
Weatherby, of Weatherby Rifle's, was a Mountain
Dweller. When she came down upon the poor
folks and soon found she liked slumming and
before long was hooked on drugs. She and my
buddy, Robert Taylor, were robbing gas stations
in LA to feed their lifestyle during 1969.

This is his story; neither elaborated nor detailed,
neither confirmed nor denied, and mostly not
true; this is just simply the lie that tells a truth.

Gavotte

Barbara's father manufactured fine, high quality, extremely expensive rifles in Germany that were known worldwide by his name. Barbara was visiting Los Angeles and was already using heroin when she met Bob at a party in Beverly Hills. Almost immediately, Bob fell in love with Barbara. Her heroin use was not a problem since he had experimented with drugs himself and was willing to try whatever she asked him to try to please her. Before long, Bob too, was addicted to heroin.

A black man Bob met from South-Central introduced Bob to a street dealer who was able to supply his and Barbara's heroin needs, but Bob quit his job to spend all his time with Barbara, and although Barbara had a substantial allowance, it was not enough to keep up with the continuing demands of both their heroin habits. They were always short of cash, and the street dealer did not deliver drugs on promises to pay.

They ran out their credit cards and hocked everything they could get their hands on, and when nothing was left, they began to borrow and to steal until no one was left to borrow or steal from. Barbara would have sold herself on the street for money, but Bob wouldn't hear of it. Instead, they decided to rob gas stations.

There had been a gun, but they had

hocked it, and so Bob walked into the gas station with no gun and his hand inside an empty paper bag. He pointed the bag at the clerk behind the counter and demanded money, while Barbara sat out front with the motor running in the Rolls-Royce sedan leased for her use by her father's corporation. The police found them afterwards together passed out naked in a motel room bed. They had left the Rolls parked in the motel's parking lot in front of their room running.

In consideration of Barbara's family connections, the District Attorney's Office dropped the charges against Barbara for her promise to enter a drug rehabilitation program designed for rich people in Switzerland. Bob was charged with armed robbery and pled guilty, believing it would keep Barbara out of prison if he accepted the blame. The judge sentenced him to eight years at San Quentin. Under the 85% law, Bob would be eligible for parole in six-years and seven-months.

Bob did not hear from Barbara and could not forget her nor accept the fact she was not trying to get in touch with him. He read about her being in Rome, amid rumors of marriage to a famous film producer. Bob did not believe it. He continued to tell anyone, who would still listen, about Barbara and that the prison mailroom was keeping her letters from him.

The Monday following Christmas week, during Bob's second year on the yard at San Quentin, he saw a picture in THE STAR of Barbara with a rock star in London. It must have been the way she was smiling and holding on to the guy that finally finished tipping the scales against Bob.

He bought eleven, twenty-dollar stamps of Mexican brown off the yard. The heroin came in little cellophane packets, and alone in his cell, Bob laid out all the packets in a neat line on the end of his bunk where he could easily reach the heroin while sitting on the toilet in the corner of the cell at the head of the bed.

He cooked the packets one at a time in a metal Coke cap over a Bic lighter flame. He got as far as the fifth packet. The guard found him at the 9:30 count. He was sitting on the toilet, leaning with one shoulder against the wall, his left arm tied off with his belt, the needle still hanging in his arm; the six packets of heroin he had not needed to kill himself still sat in a neat line on the end of his bunk.

Barbara never heard what happened to Bob. She was in Edinburgh at the time with her old crowd. There was really nothing they couldn't forget or forgive Babs, and they all had tickets to the New Year's Party at the castle. It was the place to be on New Year's Eve.

Paul Ferguson

VOICES

Of course this is more than he punishment he deserves.

Voices

Voices

Pribble stood under the tin roof of the high, open-sided work shed, looking out across the prison yard to the cellblock. Through the pouring cascade along the roof's eaves and freezing, gray drizzle, he saw dozens of other prisoners milling about, grouping together in front of the cellblock's entrance. The huge iron doors remained closed until exactly 4:30 – another three minutes – while the prisoners shivered and stamped their feet, slapping their arms against the wet and cold, their yellowish canvas coats dark, soaked through with rain.

Pribble at seventy-three years old felt the dampness in his bones. A black stocking cap covered his white hair and was pulled down low above filmy blue eyes set in a long face beside a straight nose above a wide and thick mouth and grizzled chin. The bulky canvas coat caused him to look stout and squarely built but in fact he was lean, with long straight limbs and narrow shoulders. There was little flesh on him, offering no protection against the cold and hard wind that even under the shed blew in all directions at once. He pulled the narrow coat collar up around his ears, hunching deeper into whatever cover it afforded.

The cellblock doors opened. Nodding absently, he watched with narrowing eyes the shoving rush the prisoners made for the opening doors. In a moment they had mostly disappeared inside the building. He shoved his hands deeper into the roomy coat pockets, preparing to cross the yard to the cellblock. He knew better than to hurry. His legs would only travel so fast. He hesitated a moment in front of the curtain of water that dripped from the roof edge. Still not hurrying, he leaned through it on to the yard, hearing the water pelt his hat and coat with hard, splattering drops. The wind quickened in the open, the drizzle stinging his face with tiny ice crystals. On reaching the iron doors, going through the rotunda into the gloomy shadows of the cavernous cell block, he unbuttoned his coat, welcoming the dry, if not much warmer air that greeted him. He pulled the wet cap from his head, his hair sticking straight up as he shoved the cap away in a coat pocket.

He didn't look directly at the usual hard cases along the wall, his peripheral vision noting their stiff faces and alert eyes. His age set him apart, but gave him no assurances he was immune from their violence. In a riot it was always the old men, the easy prey they killed, building their reputations while taking few risks with their own lives. During his ten years in prison, he had survived several riots. Usually by remaining in his cell and staying well away from the rioters. Others he knew had not been so lucky. He could feel the hard cases' eyes on his back as he crossed the floor to the steel stairs that climbed up and up to the top tiers of the cellblock.

He lived in cell R-26, just off the first landing. The rubber heels of his state issued clodhopper shoes rang on the stairs. Half way up the first eight of the sixteen steps he had to climb, he stopped, resting a long moment, catching his breath. His hand, placed on the rail, was cracked, the fingers twisted with large knotty joints and hard, yellowed nail. Almost useless for gripping the rail. He glared at the stairs before him as if facing an old enemy. After another long moment, he attempted to curl his fingers around the rail and continued. He stopped again on the landing. The sudden shrilling of the 5:00 lockup bell rang in his ears.

The bells woke him up in the morning. They told him when to leave his cell for the mess hall. When to report to his job on the yard. When to go to lunch and supper. And when to return to his cell to be locked up for the night. He didn't have to think. Only to know what the bells meant.

He followed the rail to the next flight of stairs and turned left, moving down the cement walk in front of the seemingly endless row of cell bars. The overhang of the next walk up was above him. There was another overhang above that. And another. And another. On and on. Eight walks high. Shelf upon shelf, tier upon tier, cell upon cell. An unbelievable weight of manmade caves, of concrete and steel, whose caged occupants clamored day and night in shrieking echoes that rebound from the furthest reaches of the great work in a reverberating roar of shame. It took some getting used to. Pribble was used to it so that he barely notices the voices without listening and could turn them on and off almost at will.

Most of the cell doors he passed were already closed and locked. A single prisoner occupied each of the four by eight cells. Through the bars he saw them sitting or lying on their bunks or sometimes standing at the sinks, or with their backs to him emptying their bladders in the toilets. Sometimes they had earphones on their heads, listening to radios or watching televisions, the appliances sitting on the floors of the cells or on shelves built onto the far end of the bunks. Because Pribble kept to himself and had never been a criminal in all his life – though he had killed his wife and was serving a life sentence – he knew few of these men. He pretended not to look into the cells and didn't speak or nod when the prisoners looked through the bars as he hurried past. He didn't appear tired, though he slid his crooked fingers along the rail, occasionally supporting his weight as he stopped to catch his breath.

Beyond the rail, fifteen feet away to the wall, the metal rods and gears, the means of opening and closing the tall row of high, wide windows, was built into the walls between the wooden casements. The windows looked out on the yard, but were now filled with the gray of the drizzling rain. It didn't matter, the glass was itself gray with dirt and hard to see through. Many panes were broken or missing. The windows were often the target of the frustration that rippled through the prison. Moist drafts breezed into the building through the openings, finding their way to the cells, which were always cold. Pribble felt the chill with pain in his hands and shoulders and across his back as he went on down the walk.

Midway along the rows of bars, he reached his own cell, twenty-six. He'd left the light burning when leaving his cell. Through the bars, he immediately saw the small ceiling bulb had been on all day. He swung open the heavy door, entered, and pulled the bars closed behind him.

A turnkey, like Pribble, another prisoner, came running. He locked the door, the key clacking loudly in the turning lock. Pribble stood watching, removing his coat. Neither of them spoke and the turnkey left.

Pribble dropped the coat on the bunk. He sat down beside it. He removed his shoes, placing them together under the bunk. He stood up in his white socks on the cold cement floor and undressed to his skivvies. He shivered, expecting to be cold. The same thing every night. He needed to hurry. He hung the green prison uniform shirt and trousers on a peg in the wall under a wooden shelf at head level across the back of the cell. He bent and picked up the coat, hanging it in place beside the uniform. The shelf contained his toiletries, and a radio and earphones. A plastic mirror was built into the wall between the shelf and sink. He had to stoop to watch himself brushing his teeth. He still had good teeth. All his own! He needed to shave. His chin looked like it had patches of snow on it. He rubbed the stubble. Shaking his head, as if shamed at being so lazy, he shrugged. At his feet a pile of books was stacked against the back wall under the sink and up beside the toilet. He no longer bothered with them. They were covered with dust.

He ran water over the toothbrush and set it back on the shelf. Wiping his mouth with his wet hand, he turned and hit the light switch. The bulb, dying, left the cell in twilight. It was not yet six o'clock. He pulled the blanket down, climbing into the bed. The sheets were cold. His feet, towards the bars, with socks on, were cold. The toilet was only two feet from his face, but it was safer to sleep with his head at that end. A few germs were nothing. A prisoner on another tier had slept with his head against the bars and someone had walked by on the walk and shot him in the back of the head with a twenty-two bullet from a zip gun. The guards hadn't caught the killer. So no one knew why, except that the head had been there and so had the zip gun. Pribble pulled the blanket up across his nose to just below his eyes. He shivered, almost trembling, waiting for his body to warm the bed.

After a little while he was content to lay still, unmoving. He listened to the voices. The prisoners pressed their faces against the cell bars. In their need to convince themselves they were not alone, their pleas mingled into an echoing roar, like that of a hungry animal. The voices comforted Pribble with the knowledge they were not in his head since they came from the surrounding cells. He could turn them off and had a simple trick now for controlling the other voices, the ones he heard that weren't real and that got inside his head before prison, and couldn't be controlled until now.

The picture of the house, or maybe its setting, allowed him control over the voices in his head. He'd been near crazy. Had been crazy. He could admit it now. Stumbling blind in the dark without a light until he'd discovered the picture. He couldn't explain its effect on him. It was just paper. No magic involved. No unknown forces. Yet, it had claimed him and continued to claim him. He thought it had everything to do with the way it connected to his former life. He closed his eyes, remembering he'd found it in an old <u>LOOK</u> magazine. In a vague sort of way, in spite of the fog in his head, he'd recognized it. But recognition hadn't been necessary. Its beauty had surprised and stirred him. The aesthetics, a surreal balance, once so familiar to him and now so foreign, had caused him to tear out the page and paste it on the ceiling of the cell where it was now. He opened his eyes, lifting them. They settled on the picture.

The orange cylinder shaped house, like a giant metal storage tank, with a flat roof and many windows of stars and quarter moons, and a round, always open, entry, was surrounded by a moat and had been photographed against a sunny background of blue sky and distant, white clouds, while pillow-like boulders flowed around the moat's steep, red banks. The sun silvered graciously spaced cottonwoods and willows that draped over the banks, shaded a wide manicured lawn of lush, vividly green grass. He knew the caption at the bottom of the page by heart, declaring it home to a New Delhi poet.

There was no cell, nor prison, and no voices in his own head. He stood in his own yard among the trees. He was sixty-three years old. His full head of white hair was wavy and fell to his shoulders. His face was lean and still strong, clean shaved, and his black eyes, though troubled, were clear under heavy, dark, brows. He looked well and not unhappy, but he was losing his mind. He didn't know why it was happening, but it was. It had been happening for some time. He'd sought professional help. Nothing had really worked, or else had worked and left him worse off. The voices – which had been so loud he'd thought others were pretending not to hear them – had stopped after the shock treatments, almost as if they had never existed; except their absence left a nagging emptiness, like a black hole where all sorts of memories and thoughts – half formed and never finished – were sucked up and lost forever in the echoing emptiness. He could feel what was left moving closer and closer to the hole and the voices were still there hiding around some other dark corner. They weren't gone. And now he was convinced that once his memories were gone his head would implode, leaving a bloody stump of spine between his shoulders. He knew it was impossible, which made it harder to accept, since he believed it was also enviable.

He knew nothing about the other voices and nothing of the missing constant pain in his hands. His fingers were long and straight, the nails clean, neatly trimmed, and pink. He had good reliable hands. And now he had no use for shoes. For one thing, he couldn't remember how to tie them, and even the huaraches he sometimes wore, driving the jeep, during his infrequent trips into town felt heavy and huge. And lately, he was full of eccentricities. Among other things, he was claustrophobic. He hated stairs and locks. Crowds frightened him. He wouldn't eat food that touched other foods. Western dress disgusted him. He preferred the freedom of dashiki tunics, tailored of white serge and long, draping to his ankles, so that now as he walked through the sun-dappled shade of the willows with his long white hair and in his white robe, he seemed almost to float, moving with the apparent serenity of a priest or holy man.

A bemused smile touched his lips. He had always been aware of the image he presented with its projected calm, denying his troubled spirit. He had traded on the image. Never hesitating to use the lie to sell himself or his work. It had meant the difference between success and failure as a poet and lecturer. The image, another little contradiction, a gift, from a God he'd never believed existed, and with all the misery in the world, couldn't accept or believe could be so cruel as to actually exist. He stopped and stood in the grass along the moat, listening to the babbling waters while looking up into the blue sky. He deeply breathed the fresh air of a miraculous day, denying its nonexistent creator.

He heard his wife, Ann, come out of the house. Turning, he folded his arms to his chest, watching her walk across the lawn towards him. She held a wicker picnic basket at her side, a red bow tied around the handle. The basket looked huge beside her. She was small, almost tiny, and gold and brown, wearing a short-sleeved white cotton blouse and long, white skirt with hand sewn blue designs of birds and flowers around the hem's wide border, and white sandals. Her long blond hair was pulled back and tied. She wore no make-up. Her eyes were wide and blue and a smattering of freckles dotted the apple cheeks and pert nose of her deeply tanned face. Earlier they had argued. He didn't remember why, and it didn't matter. Lately they argued about almost everything.

She stopped in front of him. "I thought we could lunch out here," she said, her voice light and cheerful, though not without a betraying sadness, and a quiet caution lurked in her eyes. She lifted her head, carefully watching him as she offered the basket. She broadened her smile. "Would you like that?"

"You're not my nurse," he growled, rising himself to his full height, towering over her, and ignoring the basket. "Don't humor me." He was immediately sorry. He couldn't blame her for his suffering. Simply because she was so young and couldn't believe he was dying. But the sun lit her face and hesitant blue eyes where his face was mirrored, old and green. He didn't like what he knew she saw. He couldn't escape the old man's reflection with her youth and life and his disappearing future staring at him. It made him afraid and he hid his fear in being mean. He hated his cowardice. What he really wanted was to be young with her, to talk and to laugh with her, to make love with her, joyfully, here in the yard, arriving with her as one with the moment. But he was thirty years older than her and could change the weather easier than he could turn back the clock. "I'm sorry," he apologized. "Of course, we'll have a picnic. Why shouldn't we enjoy ourselves?" He gestured with his arm, raising his voice, "For tomorrow we die!" And then, weakly, "You'll enjoy it."

"Just me?" She smiled, attempting to tease him. "Oh," she said, the smile disappearing. "Oh it's all right." She awkwardly withdrew the cumbersome basket, her arms encircling it, hugging her breasts. "If you would rather not...

Have you... Have you taken your medicine?" she looked up into his eyes, knowing he hadn't. "We don't want the voices coming back."

"It's not voices. I told you. I can still <u>feel</u> them. Like an echo. The shock treatments. All those murdered brain cells. Do you suppose they die screaming? Do you think I am crazy?"

"You have to take the pills. Otherwise, we'll have to go back to hospital. Don't you remember?"

"You do," he said bitterly, as if betrayed. "I won't go back there."

Her teeth bit at her lower lip. "Will you take the medicine?"

"No. No more."

"You know you will. I have them here. You'll have to take the pills eventually. I'm trying to help you."

He shrugged, stubbornly shaking his head. He suddenly remembered her when she was a student. Remembered her in his bed. Her small, firm, golden blond, small of the back, smooth, wet, smart body, squirming, open legs, embracing, giving, taking, climbing with him from cliff to crest, again and again, taking his breath away. No wonder he'd asked her to marry him. He held out his hand. He almost never took the pills. He took them now, tossing them into his mouth and swallowing them with his own spit.

"Happy?" he asked.

"I could be," she said, "If you would do something. If you would try to work. If you could only write. Wouldn't that help? You know it would."

"Help," he repeated. "Oh sure, this morning I remembered how to tie my shoes."

"What?"

He watched it registering. She tried not to look at his feet, his bare toes sticking out from under the robe's hem.

"You're not fair," she said. "You're trying to hurt me."

"All's fair," he said.

"Is it?" Her eyes looked past him to the far side of the moat where the sun burned and simmered the air and turning the yellow field stubble gray. "I don't like this game anymore," she said.

He didn't hear her and was listening inside himself. The voices were back. They wanted to know what he really meant to her. She'd been an undergraduate at Columbia. A fan come to hear his poetry. He'd noticed her right away. Young and fresh. A rose. A rose then, and now still a rose, but a rose with thorns. Her youth constantly pricked him. He had picked her, thorns and all, as he had picked so many others before her. At first wanting no more than to be with her. It had always been like that with him. The easy coming and going with women and girls who had already been halfway to his bed before he'd spoken to them. But there had been something about her bold enthusiasm for him. The immediate intimacy of their conversations. The way they had been together. Their prolonged lovemaking. For the first time in a long time when he could no longer remember when, he'd found himself lonely, longing for her, and believing in love again. The thirty-year difference in their ages had melted away. He had known he was playing the fool. Kidding himself and her. And it had caught up with them. He couldn't pass a mirror without it shouting back at him. It was hard to love her. He was jealous of the ground under her feet, jealous of the air she breathed, knowing the end for him was close and had to come and she would go on without him. Even now, he had lost everything he'd had to offer her. He could barely stand to look at her, knowing she remembered who he had been. And if he still meant anything to her or could still possible mean anything to her, it was only because she pitied him and felt obligated to him.

He looked at her now, the voices whispering regrets and disaster.

"We'll eat here," he said indicating the grass between them at their feet. "By the moat." But as he often did, he changed his mind. "No, I think over there. Under the trees. It's cooler."

"Aren't there bugs in the trees? Isn't that why we had them sprayed? On the leaves?"

"Alright," he said, angrily. "There are bugs in the trees. And bugs in my head. Should I have them sprayed?"

"I didn't mean that. You're making it up."

"Am I crazy?"

"Are you?" she asked, her face flushing under the tan. "I'm going back to New York." She blurted it out. This weekend. Perhaps tomorrow. As soon as I can make reservations."

"You're not leaving."

Her face had stiffened. "You don't need me." Her eyes were hard. "You don't even like me."

"I love you."

"No," she shook her head. "No. You're afraid of being alone." She continued shaking her head, her blue eyes watching him. "I'm doing what's best. You know I am. I can't stay here. You, everything. The moat. Being isolated here with you. No friends. I want to go home!"

He jumped, as if she had slapped him. "It's the voices!" He waved his hands, unable to stand still. "There are no voices. You could hear them. Listen. You see. They're gone."

"How can I hear what's in your head? You need help."

"I'm not crazy!"

"You need help. I'm tired. You need a doctor. Nurses. A hospital. I've tried. You know I have."

"The crazy old man. Is that it? You afraid of the crazy old man?"

She held out the wicker basket. He took it. "I'm sorry," she said, turning to leave.

"You're not sorry."

She stopped to turn to face him. "I'll go today. I have to go. You know I do."

"You want to go."

"It's best. You know it is."

He started, realizing he was holding the basket. He flung it away. It arched up and fell, dropping to tumble side over top across the grass to pause at the edge of the moat before sliding down the bank. The stream took it, pushing it along, tipping it and flooding over it before the basket caught; the bow came undone and was crimson against the white boulders.

Ann walked back to him. She was saying something, reaching out to touch his arm. She blurred. Gray. The voices raged, shrill, roaring. Demanding he stop her. He screamed, leaping on her. His hands encircled her neck, forcing her back and down to the grass. He fell on her.

Straddling her, he pushed his thumbs hard into her soft throat. Her small fists beat at his arms and chest. She squirmed, bucking under him.

"You think I'm old," he screamed. "That you'll live forever! That I'm dying. That I'm crazy. You're crazy. It's you! You're crazy!"

He continued to scream. Ann no longer moved. Her eyes bulged, face turning green as he choked her, screaming, his good hands around her throat, shaking her lifeless body.

The five o'clock bell shrilled. He knew it was time to wake up. The breakfast bell would ring in thirty minutes. The pain in his arthritic hands throbbed as he pushed the wool blanket off. He moved stiffly, aching all over as he slowly forced his legs to carry his feet to the floor, so that he could sit on the side of the bunk. Naked, in his t-shirt and boxers, he shivered, his teary eyes closed against remembering and against thoughts of the day he faced, policing litter on the yard.

He had fallen a long way to pick up cigarette butts. He had made a mistake. He had not been dying. Now his fall would not end until he was dead. The only peace he knew was when the voices stopped. Ann would have admired his little trick for stopping the voices. She would have forgiven him and given him her blessing, even if she would not have appreciated the nightmare he had made of their lives, killing her over and over every night, but then, she could not have it all her own way. No, she had wanted the voices to stop, hadn't she?

Paul Ferguson

A FINE EXPERIENCE

I've heard preachers, after death-row executions,
say these words, praising the dead con's love of
God and courage so often now Being there are so
many executions in America, I thought if they
read a transcript they might want to strive for
some new copy. Perhaps, [*Insert Prisoner's Name*]
Awarded Posthumous Life Achievement!

A Fine Experience

The Supreme Court lifted James Horton's stay at fifteen minutes to ten and twenty minutes later, he was dead. We followed a guard through an iron gate into the courtyard where the Prison Chaplain, Ostmann, stood flanked by two guards on the stairs in front of the brick administration building, waiting for us.

Ostmann, in his mid-twenties, was younger, for some reason, than I had supposed he would be. He was wearing sunglasses, a striped short-sleeved shirt, and gray slacks. His left hand was holding a Bible with a sheet of paper on top.

After pronouncing the time of death, he bowed his head, and then read from the paper in an almost sincere – if not downright somnambulant – southern accent.

"I knew him well. We visited almost daily. We studied the Bible together. It was what he wanted. It was important to him. He accepted Christ. And was baptized! A fellow death row offender stood up with him. Right in his cell. It was very moving.

"He did not remember doing what he had done. But like all of us, he was convinced he had done it. He really did not want to live if he could do such an awful thing.

"I try to think in terms of consequences. His execution was the consequences of his life. He was always his own worse enemy. Except at the end. When he got right with God.

"Well, he is gone now. I went with him as far as they would let me go. It was a very touching and moving experience. He was an example of courage. Why, even our superintendent said it was one of the finest experiences he has ever has ever witnessed. Of course, the Superintendent's help made it easier. Easier for us all. A fine experience. We are all grateful to the Superintendent.

"This is only my third execution as chaplain. It will always make my work here easier, knowing what a fine experience it can be. I don't believe there is any place in life among rational beings for punishing one another. I take the Bible very seriously. 'Vengeance is mine sayeth the Lord.'"

– –

When he finished we weren't allowed any questions out of respect for the families.

The guard led us back out of the prison through the iron gates. Lonnie had footage of the prison and of the reporters in the courtyard, listening to Ostmann.

As we walked to the remote-unit, Lonnie mumbled softly, so only I could hear, "Yes, sur. We killed the dum-soma-bitch, and it was a fine and moving experience, yes, sur, A *fine* experience!"

That was while I was still in Texas. KGWB–
Channel 43. They were all crazy down there. I was
glad to get away from them.

Paul Ferguson

IMAGINATION IS MAGIC

Sometimes the impossible takes a little longer.

Imagination Is Magic

Stan, in his purple silk pajamas, sat at the kitchen table. He was stooped shouldered and balding with a pale, heavily bearded face. Pamela, following their morning's routine, sat a cup and saucer in front of him on the table, then held a steaming glass pot over the cup and carefully poured it full.

He sniffed the nutty aroma, wishing the black liquid tasted as good as it smelled, but a great cup of coffee was a rare thing.

"Thanks," he said, his lips not moving as he lifted the cup.

Pam seemed not to hear. She turned away with him watching her. She returned the half empty pot to the coffeemaker on the counter. She wore a white blouse and shorts, tight around her rounded hips, showing off her long, perfectly tanned legs. She picked her own cup from beside the brewer, and turned, facing Stan as she lazily leaned with her back against the counter.

Her blonde hair, cut short in a pageboy, her red lipstick applied just so, her blue eyes perfectly drawn, came together above the cup's rim. She looked past Stan to the sun-drenched backyard outside the breakfast room windows.

250

At thirty-eight, she was still a handsome woman. Attractive and active, Stan thought. He was proud of her, and sometimes amazed, wondering how she managed to take care of him and the house and to exercise while making a success of the antiques store she had opened on Peachtree Street, downtown. She was not only his wife whom he loved, and his best friend, much admired; she was also his main link (as such things were once said of husbands) to the world.

He was a writer of adventure tales and working at home over the years he'd become engrossed in his work, leaving Pam to deal with the butcher, the baker, the candlestick maker, anyone and anything that might distract him. Until recently, it had been a happy arrangement and he'd thought her happy and content with their lives looking forward to the future. They shared a taste for travel to far away places and had talked about purchasing a sailboat, sailing the Pacific Rim, visiting Japan and China and sailing among the islands, their imaginations conjuring images of balmy days on blue lagoons and moonlit nights on exotic beaches. Now, or at least soon, their dreams would be possible.

Stan's latest novel was on the Time's bestsellers list and there was a movie contract. All the years of hard work were finally paying off, but there was a catch. Pam was having an affair.

He knew when it started, six weeks earlier. The impressions of unfamiliar numbers on a phone pad. Notes discovered in her purse while digging out the car keys. Assignations: a motel's name and room number written in a masculine scribble, a matchbook cover from the town's only rock and roll club, a place he'd never set foot in. It all obviously added up, although there wasn't enough proof positive, except. He'd seen them together. The antique store was closed on Wednesday and the meetings continued every Wednesday afternoon from week to week.

He doubted it was anything more than a fling. It hadn't happened before, not that he knew, and he believed he would have known, just as he knew now. He also doubted Pam would leave him. Her lover was a new man in town and to risk letting the affair run its course, betting his life the guy wouldn't fall in love with Pam or Pam with him. Stranger things have happened. So the problem was the end of the affair for them and for himself. The sooner the better.

It was a tricky situation. Dueling fortunately was illegal, and publicly humiliating himself wasn't Stan's thing. He couldn't slug the guy and no good would come of confronting him or Pam. Even if he'd had evidence and had photographed the meetings, which he hadn't, Pam would never admit anything and he had never won an argument with her. She would never forgive him. Besides, she possessed the ultimate weapon. He'd played the scene out in his head. Between denials, she would cry heart-rendering sobs, and the tears would be enough to break his heart. He could see himself giving in, making excuses for her, apologizing for having ever doubted her, wanting to believe her, and finally believing her. No, he needed a different approach. Something clever and subtle, bringing her back to him and he thought he had.

The coffee scalded his tongue. Swallowing, he told her, "I'm losing my imagination."

"Sugar Bear," she said, looking at him over the top of her cup, "you're the most imaginative man I know."

He sighed, shaking his head. "No, this is serious. Can you sit down for a minute?"

"It's Wednesday. You know I've got a tennis date."

"Who's it with," he asked, forgetting his purpose wasn't to argue, "the pro?" The newly hired blonde athlete was working his way through the roster of member's wives.

"Marge," she answered. "I thought you said you were losing your imagination."

"That doesn't take much. The guy can't keep his pants on,"

"Thanks loads," she said. "Is that what you think of me?"

"You know who I mean."

"Sara? Not again. I swear, Sugar Bear, you're obsessed with her and Morty."

Sara Rosenthal had run away with the country club's former tennis pro. Stan felt sorry for Morty, her husband. Poor guy was dying of a broken heart. Amazingly, Morty hadn't seen it coming. Sara wasn't what Stan would have called the perfect wife. She'd always been a bit too social with the younger set. In particular, the husbands. There had been rumors. Pam had known, telling Stan, and Morty should have guessed.

Stan hadn't deliberately brought Sara into the conversation, but the coincidental mention of her pleased him. He hoped Sara might have bred guilt by association, if that was possible, since she and Pam had been friends. Perhaps the thought would penetrate Pam's defenses. It worked in his novels. Of course, he sometimes fudged, and Pam simply left the kitchen. So, he thought, reality made the difference. Then again, perhaps not. She was moving around in the bedroom. Definitely feeling the pressure.

He didn't feel guilty himself. He was improvising, using what was at hand, and smiled to himself, feeling pleased. Guilt had its place and for most of history had kept women at home and husbands returning to them. Now, with the shoe, as they say, on the other foot, he clearly saw its purpose and knew because of it, round one was his in a fight to the finish. No quarter given. He was the only one fighting.

He wasn't at all being fair and wasn't about to cash in twelve years of marriage by playing fair. To survive he had to adapt or go the way of the dinosaur. He remembered first seeing her. She had worked as an editor for his New York publishers. She'd been cool, efficient, and beautiful. Her high heels had clicked against the marble floor of the cramped, book-filled, Fifth

Avenue office, her strong calves tightening in her good legs with those good thighs and rounded buttocks stressing the fabric of her skirt. He'd physically been attracted to her immediately. But it was her blue stocking mind, a word scratched here, added there, pages moved, demands made on him and his work that had given him reason to admire her. It hadn't taken him long to fall in love and it hadn't hurt anything that like him she was originally from Atlanta, a Georgia girl. Like so many southern beauties she'd run away north, looking for her dreams, and he'd believed she would want to return home and had been certain they were a matched set. He'd been right. Although it had taken him nearly a year and most of his savings with monthly, sometimes weekly flights between Atlanta and New York, wining and dining her, using every bit of wit and charm and persuasion he possessed, before she had agreed to marry him.

He'd brought her home to the house where he'd been raised in the suburbs south of Atlanta and had felt like he had won the Nobel Prize. He'd never doubted her. She had sacrificed her career for a future with him, though she had continued to edit his work. Her touch was present in everything he did, providing the encouragement and discipline he needed and often lacked. With Pam beside him, approving of him, his writing had taken on a clarity and depth he had hardly recognized. It was her gift to him, and as it turned out, her gift to them both. His sales steadily increased.

If there was any sadness in their lives, it was that they couldn't have children. And even this was more to himself than her. Her parents were dead and he was the last of his line. She seemed perfectly happy the way things were without the complications of children. But the glow had faded with him being wrapped up in his writing and neglecting her, taking her and their lives for granted, so that now he didn't blame her for going in search of what they had lost. He supposed it was natural, and if he could win her back, he wouldn't make the same mistake again.

She came out of the bedroom. He watched her walk towards him. She was carrying her canvas tennis bag, the racket pushed between the leather handles. She'd tied her blue sweater around her waist, draped behind her, covering her hips. She stopped at the table and pulled out a chair and sat down. Dropping the back on the floor between their chairs, she propped her elbow on the table, resting her chin on her hand.

"Here, I'm all yours," she said.

"What about your date?"

"Hurry."

He hadn't thought this far ahead, though he had thought and thought; now he hesitated, searching for words. He began slowly, uncertain. "I'm not messing around. Something happened to me."

He lifted his cup, sipping from it.

"Am I supposed to guess?"

"No," he shook his head, beginning again, trying to know, without knowing, what he should say. "Last week I was downtown, stopped in the car on Broad Street, at the light outside Turner's Drugs, and ... I don't know.... Well, first, I'd been thinking about it. You know, about losing my imagination. And there's more to it. As if someone has deleted a file and I don't now what or who. Only that its not there."

He fell silent. She wasn't looking at him. Her gaze went past him, through the window to the backyard. He turned his head, looking out. The crimson against the silvering green of leaf and thorn. The hybrid Bermuda, so common to the upper-middle class neighborhood lawns, grew thick in the black mulch beneath the rose bushes and was tall with yellowing tips along the side and back of the sun-faded redwood fence. A sparrow dropped down into the grass, gave a hop, and flew away.

He turned back to her. "I want you to listen," he told her. "Look at me. This is important. Either that or I'm losing my mind."

"Sugar Bear, you're not losing your mind," she said, looking at him. "You're thirty-nine years old. You're healthy. You've got a nice home, a beautiful wife, and you're talented and successful. They lock up crazies and give them none of the above." She smiled impatiently. "If that's all, I have to go."

"No, no," he said hurriedly. "I haven't told you anything. That's not all. How can it be? I – These things are connected. You're part of it.

You know what I mean? I can't work without my imagination. It would be like working without you. You know that don't you?"

"Don't be silly."

"You know, don't you?"

"Well, I'm here."

"Yes," he said with genuine sadness. "I know, but something is missing."

"What's wrong?"

"Everyone looks alike."

"What?"

"Haven't you noticed?"

"Noticed?"

"You haven't seen it?"

"That everyone looks alike?" She muffled a sound in her palm. "You're serious," she said, lowering her hand to look at him.

"You think it's funny." He had to control his voice, the words hissing out between his teeth. "For God's sake, Pam, I'm a writer!"

"No," she agreed. "It isn't funny."

"Okay."

"Maybe you should see Joe," she said, her friend, the analyst.

"It's not in my head. I mean it is. Of course it is, but not like that."

"She sighed. "Okay," she said. What started all this?"

He sat for a long moment, studying her. She dropped her eyes, lifting them to look through the window. He wondered what she saw. The fence? The sky? Or something she wanted and was thinking about? The afternoon's interlude and maybe being late?

She was an energetic lover. He wondered did she bounce and roll, naked in her lovers arms, as she did in his, and would the motel bed, as theirs did, constantly groan, threatening collapse? But such thoughts led nowhere and were dangerous. He pushed them out of his mind. He had to save, not destroy their marriage.

"You won't be late," he said, hearing the bitterness in his own voice. She gave him a sharp look and he let out a long breath. "Everything is connected," he said. "They can divide a subatomic particle and put half in Australia and half in Texas. Punch one and the other jumps. It doesn't matter how far apart they are. They don't know why, but it's changing how we see the universe. It's changing everything. So, maybe, the earth was flat until that guy Columbus changed it."

Pam frowned. "It was always round."

He shook his head. "I just mean we effect what we see. It affects us. I saw something."

He despaired of continuing. He had to be obvious. Pam was no dummy. He wondered how obvious could he be before it blew up in his face.

"Is there any point to any of this?' she asked.

Again, he searched for words, determined to continue. His hand unconsciously rubbed his bearded chin. "I was downtown and had been thinking about how things are connected. How each of us has created the world, filling in things and places, even peoples faces with our imagination. You know I play with ideas. It's what I do. Then I was stopped at the red light in front of Turner's, and just as it turns green, I look across the street at the oncoming traffic. Just one car. A gray, vague sort of thing without any markings. A roadster like Plymouth makes, but hardtop, stopped at the corner. Do you see? No markings?

"Anyway, a man was driving with a woman in the seat beside him. She was scooting down, hiding herself. She didn't want to be seen, but I saw her. I wish I hadn't. And the man too. Now, Pam, don't laugh. This is the hard part. You'll have to trust me. They didn't... I don't know how to say it. They didn't have faces. No –"

"Why are you telling me this?" she demanded, interrupting him. Her face was flushed and she had lifted her chin from her hand, leaning away from him. "You think it was me?"

"What? No, no. You were at the club."

"You know I was," she said. Her hands trembled and she dropped them out of sight to her lap below the table. "I'm always at the club on Wednesday. You can call me."

"Well, I didn't see them. That's just it," he said, studying her. She was breathing heavily. Her blue eyes and red lips stark against her pale face. "You see," he added, "that's what I'm telling you."

She looked confused. "You didn't see them?"

"Weird, huh? They didn't have faces."

"I don't understand."

"Their faces were gone. I couldn't fill them in."

"I still don't…"

"I told you. I'm losing my imagination. I couldn't create a face for them. You see?"

"Why are you doing this?"

He shook his head, ignoring her question. "Maybe I'm going blind?"

"You're not going blind." She cleared her

throat, straightening in the chair. "They had faces. What about the car?"

"No markings. You see?"

"Maybe it was new. You're being silly. The sun shining on the car widows. You probably couldn't see. That's it, isn't it? It happens, doesn't it? The glare?"

"Was the sun even out?"

"Yes," she said.

"I know what I saw."

"You didn't see anything. You just said you didn't."

"Yes, but…"

"It's nothing. You're all right now?

"Oh, because you're here, but what happens when I'm alone and turn into HAL? You know, Clarke's computer? 'Daisy, Daisy, give me your answer, do' Grrrrr."

A light seemed to come on behind her eyes. The color returned to her cheeks. She visibly brightened. Leaning towards him, she smiled. Her sudden laughter, a pretty sound, surprised him. She was heartbreak beautiful. "You don't have to worry," she said, "I'm here."

His heart turned over, beating fast. He

had to pretend to ignore the change in her. "You are, aren't you?"

"I'll always be here," she said, her voice sweet and clear.

"But, Pam…"

She stood up. Pushing back her chair, she quickly came around the table. She folded her arms around his balding head and drew his face to her breasts. The soft smell of her enveloped him. Her breath was warm, her lips hot, almost feverish, pressed to the top of his head.

"I'm here," she soothed him, the whispered words sending good chills down his spine and radiating to his hips.. He put an arm tight around her hips, pulling her close against him. "What about your date?"

"I'm not going."

"No?"

"No. They'll just have to play without me."

"As long as I don't," he said, nuzzling against her.

"You won't."

"And I won't turn into the computer HAL, will I?"

"Never," she said, kissing the top of his head again and again and again. "Never, never, never…"

Paul Ferguson

THE OLD MAN

I had this guy for ten years. My buddy owned him
for five years before he was mine. Most of the
story happened – the scouting of the yard is true –
and I have a picture of us here with me.
Sometimes, values apply no matter which type
animal you happened to have been born.

The Old Man

The Old Man lived fifteen years. He was a Polish gaming rooster who started life in a cage owned by a cock-fighter with a pit in the woods across the Alabama River from Selma.

I never saw the Old Man fight. According to my pal Roger Johnson, the Old Man was a favorite in the pit, and of course he survived, which, without anything more, says an awful lot about him.

In some ways, I suppose Roger and I based our appreciation of the Old Man as much on our own lives, the way we lived growing up, as on his life in the cage and pit. During the forties and fifties times were hard in Selma. There were not a lot of jobs and too many people, black and white, were willing to work for almost no wages, so that it was never easy for our parents to put food on the table, and every day it seemed like a struggle to survive.

Roger and I joined the Army to get away from it, but it was almost the same thing in the Army, and when we came home afterwards, nothing had changed. Then in the sixties, there were the civil rights battles and Selma was in the middle of it and things began to change. The government came to Alabama with highway projects and northern companies followed, opening factories, looking for cheap labor.

By the early 1970's there were lots of jobs. I started my own construction company and Roger became supervisor at the lock plant north of town. We each married, had children, and bought homes, Roger in Selma, me in the country. We were earning money and it seemed like a lot of money, enough to buy us into the American Dream we had always heard about, but had never believed included us.

Roger, like his father Mister Johnson, was a big cockfighting fan. After seeing the Old Man fight, Roger paid two-hundred dollars for him, and told me he intended to make a whole lot more money, fighting the Old Man in the pit, but things happen. The state Alcohol, Tax and Firearms agents raided the cockfights, and Roger, abandoning cockfighting, turned the Old Man loose in the backyard behind the house.

There were no more fights nor cages, nor ropes to tie the Old Man's legs, staking him out in the cock-fighters junk strewn yard between fights. Roger talked me into helping him build a coop, about the size of a large doghouse with an open front and broom handles across it for perches. Roger bought half a dozen mixed Cornish and Bantam hens. The old man was free with his own house and harem. He must have thought he had died and gone to paradise.

Roger spent hours, just sitting in the backyard, drinking beer, and watching the Old Man. The admiration might have been mutual. Roger would whistle and the Old Man would fly up and perch on Roger's out held arm.

The Old Man

I first saw him do that in 1978, Roger's broad dark face, beaming with a proud smile, while the old man sat on his out held arm. After seeing them together like that, and thinking about it, and about our lives, I sort of figured we all deserved a happy ending.

During the next few years not much changed. Life for us was good, but of course, the one certainty everyone shares in life is that life is what happens to you; there are no certainties. The animal control people in Selma decided to start enforcing the law against keeping livestock in the city limits.

Roger asked me to take the Old Man and his flock out to my place. I have a picture taken the day they arrived. The Old Man is perched on Roger's arm. Black body with white spotted wings, a yellow ruff, and long, iridescent blue-black tail feathers, he is stretched up on his toes with his head cocked to the side, looking into Roger's black eyes, as if asking what all the fuss was. It was not like Roger was losing the Old Man, we spent most of our time together anyway.

At the time, I was building a new barn and paddocks and we threw up a fenced coop to keep the Old Man and his hens from underfoot. Then, with the barn finished, we built them a real nice, proper coop at the side of the barn with nesting boxes for the hens and a door with a little ramp to the yard, so that the Old Man could come and go without being penned up.

During the next five years I saw for myself what Roger meant about the way the Old

Man watched his hens, getting them up and out to the yard in the morning, and shepherding them back to the coop in the evening, leaving no doubt among them, or for me, that he was doing the best he could for them.

It was easy to see what the Old Man thought important, and watching him made me feel good about myself and my own life and family. There was an order to things that seemed natural and right and I began thinking of the Old Man as a friend, and now when I whistled, he would fly up and perch on my out held arm.

In 1985, a business opportunity called me and my family to a construction project in Arizona. It meant more money than I had ever earned. The wife and I decided to sell our place and buy a new, maybe bigger place when we returned. We had to arrange board for all the animals, and Roger proved to be of little or no help. I almost think he would have preferred me to stay and miss the opportunity. He did nothing to make our leaving easier. There was the Old Man and the hens, the kids' ponies, and the dogs and the cows and even Bill, our goat. I could have used Roger's help, finding suitable places to board them, but somehow the wife and I managed without him.

I left the Old Man with my cousin in Perry County, promising to pick him up when we returned. We were gone until 1988. Then, with the project finished, a friend in Phoenix offered to sell us his place in north Florida. It was exactly what we wanted; fifty-four acres with a house and a barn, and it was a steal at the price. We took it, moved back, and began reassembling our lives. This, naturally, meant picking up what remained of our livestock, dogs, horses, ponies, cows, our goat, Bill, and finally, the Old Man and his hens. Florida would not have been home without our animals.

The barn on the new place was huge, with twenty-seven horse stalls and five paddocks, and was roughly one-hundred yards from the house. The Old Man quickly took it over. There were now more than a dozen mostly new hens in his flock, but he himself never seemed to age. He never acted or looked any different, or older, but he had acquired a sidekick at my cousin's farm, a little, white Bantam rooster who seemed now to be second in command and who was seldom far from the Old Man's side.

They had the run of the place and made the most of it. In the evening, coming home from work, I would sit out on the side deck and watch them in the barnyard beyond the split rail fence that surrounded the house. The white Bantam, as the sun would begin to set, would do most of the herding, moving the hens toward the barn, the Old Man slowly following, hanging back, always last, and then lingering just outside the wide barn doors until the first stars appeared in the darkening twilight sky.

The lock plant in Selma closed and Roger took his retirement, sold his house in Selma and moved to Milton, Florida, twenty miles west of our place. We did not see as much of each other as we had hoped. I was busy, often on the road with work, and he had taken a job at Wal-Mart in

Milton. Our kids were grown now, and we had grandchildren, and they took up a lot of time, visiting them in Pensacola, driving back and forth, and Roger's children and grandchildren were still in Selma, so he was gone a lot of weekends. We were still close, but mostly, barely able to get together every other weekend and holidays with both families visiting at my place. I guess our families and jobs had really always come first, and now that we're older, they filled our lives. There was just not as much time as there had been when we were younger. We still enjoyed watching the Old Man, and I suppose we thought we knew everything about him, but, in fact, he never ceased to amaze us.

Our families spent Thanksgiving week together in 1990 at my place. We were there together when a neighbor from up the road dropped by and asked if I could keep his dog, a Great Dane, over the weekend. He had company and their little kids were afraid of the huge dog. I had big dogs myself and did not think his would be a problem, and agreed to watch the Dane, telling the neighbor to tie the dog to a tree behind the house. Later, after dark, with flashlights in hand, Roger and I went back to check on the Dane and discovered he had killed one of the Old Man's hens. While Roger loaded the dog in his pickup and returned him to the neighbor, I buried the hen.

Early the next morning, the sun barely peeking over the distant treetops beyond the still misty hay fields, Roger and I, sitting together on the side deck, having our coffee, saw the Old Man and his Bantam sidekick come out of the barn.

271

They were alone, although normally the hens would have been with them. It was the flocks habit to start the day searching and pecking for bugs in the grass around the house. Roger and I had discussed and dismissed the Dane and dead hen, and so they were not on our minds, and we were only mildly curious as to why the Old Man and Bantam were crossing the barnyard this morning without the hens.

As we watched, they came on over and stopped just beyond the split rail fence. There was something nervous, expectant, and cautious about the way they moved, pausing, and jerking their heads from side to side, before finally darting forward and ducking under the lowest fence rail into the yard. I looked at Roger, but he only shrugged as we continued to watch them disappear at the front of the house, moving around the far side, before eventually coming back around from behind the house to where we could again observe them as they crossed in front of the deck to approach the fence where they had entered the yard. The Bantam then slipped under the lowest rail and headed back in the direction of the barn while the Old Man stood a long moment, watching him, before, with a silent flip of his spotted wings, he flew up to settle on the top most rail, his head cocked, and beady eyes hard with suspicion. In the interim, the sidekick had disappeared into the barn to quickly reappear, leading the hens across the barnyard to where the Old Man flew down from the fence to join them before leading them under the fence and into the yard in front of us.

Maybe Roger and I were just a couple of

small town hicks and what we saw or thought we saw was due to our own ignorance and interpretation, but my face must have mirrored Roger's delight as we suddenly burst out laughing. The Old Man had scouted the yard, looking for the Dane. Then, deciding the dog was gone, that the yard was safe, he had sent his sidekick to bring the hens back. We could not have been more amazed or delighted with him, or pleased with ourselves for having witnessed the moment. Of course, we have no proof of it, or of the Old Man's intentions, but we never doubted him and had always known he was something special. Roger had long since quit eating chicken, and for a long time after that, and actually, even before that, the thought of eating anyone related to the Old Man had not agreed with my imagination.

I guess that was the last moment Roger and I shared, and I was glad we had it. He died before Christmas of a heart attack. I do not know how anyone gets over that, except to remember the way we were together. The Old Man seemed to miss our old pal, or maybe old age finally caught up with the Old Man. He died in January, sometime in the night on his roost in the barn. I found him and buried him out back next to the hen. I remembered then that I had never heard the Old Man crow. Roger had said the Old Man's throat had been torn in the fighting pit. He could not crow. I thought it a shame, as it seemed to me that if ever a rooster had anything to crow about, it was the Old Man.

AMERICA'S 48 BLOODIEST ACRES

This is from my journal. I thought it interesting enough to make a story. With all the moving from one institution to another, a lot of the journal was lost. I sent about five-hundred pages to my archive at the University of Alabama which amounts to around one-fifth of what I had when I left. All lost now.

America's 48 Bloodiest Acres

March 14th, Wednesday: Told this morning by cellblock guard, while I was still in bed, to report to the Counseling Center immediately after breakfast to see Mr. D__. He is the new superintendent. The guard didn't know what D__ wanted.

When any suit sends for me, my instinct is to worry. Suits do not hand out good news. They call you into an office and abruptly pull the rug out from under you, telling you your wife is divorcing you, or you are going back to court with new charges, or your custody level is being raised, and since they never answer your questions, obstinately insisting, 'That's all I know,' as they dismiss you from the office, you are at a loss, if not devastated, wondering what to do, or what happened, left without any answers and just a bit more destroyed than when you entered the office.

Like the guards, who insist on being called 'correctional officers,' (glorified baby-sitters,) the suits are schooled in a bullying redneck philosophy not to communicate with you, to let you worry about communicating with them, the idea being to punish, not assist, or let themselves get involved with inmates. It works. Every guard, caseworker, chaplain, nurse, doctor, or suit that follows this advice is hated to the core of their being.

D__ was the caseworker. I had never

spoken to him, but he had been pointed out to me as he crossed the yard, hurrying among the towering, fortress-like cellblocks. He was wearing a green golf-shirt and khaki trousers, the cuffs, stopping above his ankles, white socks streaking along above scuffed, black loafers. He was young, young for a superintendent, early forties, short, with stocky, thick shoulders and chest, muscular, ropy arms a trim, firm waist, a full head of black hair combed high in waves around a long, pale face with angular jaws of blue shadows. He reminded me of an elementary school gym instructor or coach, a guy with a sweaty odor like beef stew, wafting through the Old Spice. The con pointing him out, told me, "That guy has never met an inmate he couldn't hate."

It is the same with any caseworker. Their job is to keep inmate files updated. They are clerks, paper pushers, obliged to deal with inmates, but not required to actively assist them. Many caseworkers start as guards, quickly prove their incompetence, rise to sergeants, and are transferred by Custody to Administration. Some people are hired as caseworkers and have a smattering of sociology, administration or computer science, or maybe a course or two in psychology, but they are the exceptions and don't last long. A lot of caseworkers were hired because they already had family working for the DOC: fathers, mothers, husbands, wives, sisters, brothers, daughters, in-laws, cousins, all in positions to get them the job. They generally know nothing about counseling or administration, and often as not, are computer illiterate.

D__ assumed the superintendent spot by default. He was appointed acting super after the old superintendent left for Central Office. The rumors on the yard claimed the old super had been busted stealing auto parts from the state garage just outside the prison walls in order to rebuild the antique cars he collected. Central Office made the call, and makes all decisions for the thirty or so institutions, employees, and 30,000 plus inmates that comprise the DOC. No policy or procedure is enacted that Central does not approve. D__ is Central's boy, and as a caseworker was evidently good at following orders, doing nothing, but since making superintendent, he evidently thinks more is required of him. He constantly issues policy changes, which after the fact, are just constantly vetoed by Central. The result has been chaos at the prison for staff and inmates, neither knowing what rules to enforce or obey. The big boys at Central, while greedy, having complete discretion of how to slice and dice the $350,000,000.00 a year budget they receive to operate the DOC, are not necessarily stupid, although they seem to gladly suffer fools. The rumors on the yard say D__ is scheduled for bigger things, so Central puts up with him. This seems about right to me. Central does not reward competence, or anyone who might present a threat from the inside. The old super is an example. Central owns him now, if not in his slathering gratitude, then because they can trust him, knowing he knows that if he ever opens his mouth about them to the wrong people, his head will roll from the chopping block. He'll probably end up running the DOC. The one thing that protects the bosses is that no one can afford to talk, so that, one way or another, like any Mafia, silence is assured by the gun at their backs. That the rewards are money and power only increases the corruption, reassuring them, this is how the game is played.

Anyway, I was in no hurry to see D__, and ended up running late, hung up in the breakfast line. The prison had been serving only three meals a day for the last hundred-fifty years, and the civilian cooks still can't get it right. It took twenty minutes for them to notify the cooks downstairs in the kitchen to send more oatmeal upstairs to the dining room. it wasn't worth the wait, but I figured if D__ said anything about me being late, it would give me an opportunity and an excuse to complain about the consistently unidentifiable rations the cooks serve, passing them off as meals.

By the time I crossed the yard to the Center, a squat single story redbrick building with barred windows and a flat roof strung with razor wire, I was having doubts, nursing a faint hope that maybe this was good news. I couldn't think of anything I had done, and if someone outside the walls had died, the guard would have sent me to the Chapel. I decided to hope for the best, but like I said, suits are bad news.

Sure enough, I got a whiff of that Old Spice as I came through the door. D__ was seated behind Mrs. C__'s desk, just to the left. Apparently, he had appropriated the desk while waiting for me, as his office, as far as I knew, was out front in the Administration building.

Mrs. C__, with her granny glasses and silvery-gray hair, was standing among the desks of the other caseworkers through the open door into the back office. She was wearing a bright yellow, baggy sack-dress printed with big orange flowers. Mrs. C__ is a nice old lady, although a bit dim. She nodded at me with a quick smile that seemed

part frown as she turned away to the coffee maker
on the table behind her.

D__ made some slight noise in his throat,
his eyes flickering in my general direction, barely
acknowledging my presence, as without ceremony
he informed me I could not accept the P.E.N.
prize for my play, Everything That's Cool.

I felt my stomach knot. "I haven't seen
any money," I said, without thought, while trying
to think how to change his mind. "I received a
letter, notifying me I won, but the mailroom took
the check. I thought it was sent to accounting to
be put on my books."

I had written the one-act play originally at
the request of The Prison Players, a group of
inmate actors, to be performed by them on the
gym stage, but their civilian sponsor, under the
rules (something I did not know at the time), had
to submit the play to D__ for approval. He had
rejected it. The story affirms that everything even
remotely humanizing was forbidden and
considered contraband by the prison authorities.
D__'s rejection of it hadn't surprised me, but he
could not kill the play by banning its performance
inside the walls. I had sent it to the P.E.N. Writing
Contest for Prisoners, in New York. D__
probably felt P.E.N.'s recognition of the play was
a slap in the face. I didn't care if he did.
Everything That's Cool was my property. The
P.E.N. award did not change anything, no more
than D__'s rejection of the play. I think, and I
write. The results belong to me. It's how I create,
how I build, and give purpose to my existence. My
problem was that writing costs money. I needed
the award. In fact, I needed every penny I could

possibly scrounge for paper, pencils, pens, ribbons, envelopes, and postage, so that I could continue to write and send work to publishers. If this was personal for D__, for me, it was a threat to my existence. Besides, the award was mine. All the hours and days and months and years spent in my cell, writing, and finally, learning to write, had earned me whatever rewards my efforts brought. I had to convince D__, and thought there might be a way:

"It's not everyday," I pointed out, "that a prisoner writes a prize winning play. You could call the newspapers and television stations. It would make for a good public relations story for the Department of Corrections. Maybe we could get them to publish a picture in the paper of you handing me the check. The department is constantly under fire for not doing enough to rehabilitate inmates. This shows rehabilitation is happening. It's the kind of public relations story you want. It's proof," I said. "Rehabilitation has happened. Look what I've accomplished in the state's most violent prison."

He leaned forward, an elbow on the desk, his hand waving away my suggestion. "Well," he said, "you'll have to send it back."

I had given him a perfect response to the worst public criticism the DOC faced, and it had slid past him without registering.

"Do you know who these P.E.N. people are?" I asked, keeping the disgust I felt for his ignorance from rising wit the anger I was beginning to feel. I had to be careful. An inmate could talk himself into the hole simply by disagreeing with staff, and this guy was the Superintendent. "P.E.N. isn't just national," I informed him. "It's international. People like Arthur Miller, Dorothy Allison, John Updike, Salman Rushdie, belong to P.E.N. They serve on the committees that decide the awards." These were names on the P.E.N. letterhead, along with many other famous and not so famous writers. I doubted they knew I existed, but was hoping D__ would know of them. "I'm not refusing P.E.N.'s recognition of my work," I told him, meaning it. Whatever he wanted to do as a consequence of my refusal, he could do. I had been to the hole before. In fact, I had spent nearly nine months in the dark hole. "If you want to refuse the award, then you send it back. You've got the check. Get on the phone to these guys at P.E.N. in New York and explain to them why I can't accept it. Maybe P.E.N. will have something to say about me not being allowed to keep it."

He raised his head to look at me. His narrowing eyes were a dull winter's gray, and just as empty and emotionally blank as his starchy white face. "I'll have to notify Central Office," he said, his voice raspy with irritation, but with no change in his expression. "Is that what you want? You want to involve Central Office?"

"I'm not refusing the award," I said, beginning to wonder why he had to invoke Central Office. Maybe I was wrong. If he was willing to turn it over to Central, to let it decide, maybe this wasn't personal. Or maybe he was bluffing. But if this was poker, he was lousy at it. Central Office was no threat to me. All it could do was agree with him. Besides, Central had more to do than screw around with an accomplished fact. There might even be someone there who knew what they were doing. Either way, I would not be any worse off for holding my ground. It was a push, a tie, and if he turned it over to Central, it meant he would be out of the game.

We left it like that, his curt dismissal, sending me back across the yard to the cellblock, bothering me not at all.

Thursday, the 15th: Phoned Mark Allen in Nevada, and asked him to phone Jackson Taylor, the Director of P.E.N.'s writing program for prisoners, letting Taylor know what had happened here, and informing him, if I lose the battle with D__ (no way to win the war), to have Taylor send the money to me through Mark's production company in Vegas. The phone call eliminated the concern that any letters might be held up in the mailroom.

The phones, every word and grunt are recorded, then listened to. When D__'s name comes up, the recording will be played for him. He is not going to appreciate my comments about his lack of communication and public relation skills. He'll also know, sending the money back to P.E.N. will change nothing. It might even light a fire under P.E.N.'s more active members. As writers, they will know of the government's constant infringement of copyright laws and trouncing that intellectual property rights have been taking.

For over thirty years, P.E.N. supported writers in prison (and of course, out). The literary creations P.E.N. members and grants are directly and indirectly responsible for, are without number. Among other battles, in the 1970's the late Dr. Timothy Leary, Harvard lecturer, LSD guru/explorer, and writer, would have perished in the hole of a California prison, if P.E.N. members had not pro-actively involved themselves, writing articles, petitioning the parole board, and the California Governor's office; finally in 1976, forcing Leary's release from the hole and from prison by publicly demanding the parole board follow its own guidelines. I am obviously no Tim Leary, and do not expect P.E.N. or anyone else to come riding to my rescue, but I am a writer, and it doesn't hurt to hope and to act as if the possibility of P.E.N.'s help exists for me.

Friday, the 23rd: The media was not notified, but the P.E.N. award was posted to my account this morning. Do not know if D__ or Central Office is responsible. It does not much matter. I am not grateful for being ill-used or to whoever belatedly decided to do what is right.

Phoned Mark and told him. After nearly ten years of following my prison life by phone, he was not surprised.

Mark is a rock. He is also a first rank western entertainer. During our rodeo days he enjoyed hyping the paradox of being a Jewish cowboy from New York. He billed himself as "The New York Cowboy." With spinning guns, trick roping, and cracking bullwhips, he could bring any arena audience to its feet. He tells people now, if he was where I'm at, he would want a friend on the streets like himself. He is a class act, which is why we were friends in the first place. We are pals in what the old hands call "the cowboy way." In over twenty years, there has never been a single moment when I did not and since there are no real friendships, except between equals, I know Mark feels the same. There have been times when chaos and mayhem, the noise and blood, the always sudden violence, except that I could pick up the phone and call Vegas and hear Mark's voice, or else talk to Jo, his wife, and be reminded of exactly why I love life. Years ago, another friend, the late Colonel William (Bill) Noble, of Noble Wild West Shows, and his wife Ozark Annie, had somehow acquired a pair of beautifully etched, silver spurs with the big Mexican rowels and wide, somewhat worn, leather straps decorated with heavy silver concho's. A letter authenticated the spurs and was attached to a photograph of Poncho Villa mounted on a black horse, a matching spur strapped to Villa's one visible heel. Bill, recognizing my admiration for the spurs, handed me one of them, telling me to keep it. One Villa spur by itself was worth little, while together, the pair was nearly priceless. This was our friendship. I feel the same way about Mark. His friendship is beyond priceless. If he ever reads this, I hope he blushes.

He said he would phone Taylor.

Jackson Taylor may imagine I cried "wolf." The twists and turns of the endless prison maze, constructed of an irrationality of meanness, of pokes and prods, of constant attacks on the "self," by a deliberately institutionalized syndrome of prison abuse, endured by prisoners 24-7, lacks reality and commands no urgency from anyone who has not been behind the walls; even so, I'm grateful that he is there.

I am still not out of trouble. Central Office may, as far as D__ is concerned, have saved his face for now, but he won't forget, and that I've got to live with whatever he does or decides to do. They have my body, and every writer in prison I have any knowledge of who has earned any measure of public recognition, however marginal, has eventually paid for it, being moved to close security to be isolated, watched and continuously harassed. I somehow doubt that I'll be the exception.

Sunday, the 25th: My birthday. Jim Lightfeather, my Anishinabe pal, stopped by my cell. Knowing my love for chocolate he had saved his 11oz, hollow, milk chocolate Santa Claus from the prison xmas package and gave it to me. Jim shames me. I don't know his birthday.

Wednesday, the 28th: Received notice through institutional mail that prison policy forbids me conducting business through the mails, which means I can not use the mail to sell my plays and stories to publishers. This policy comes from Central Office. I am not glad for the attention and doubt Central is worried about me exploiting or being exploited by publishers. Nor is it the money. It's far more likely Central's concern is with what I am writing and to keep me from being heard. If it comes to it (and it has), I'll give my work away. I mean to keep writing.

Friday the 30th: Sent to the Center by guard to see Mrs. C__. She told me I've been transferred to a medium security prison. This was not expected. The new place has been described to me by inmates who have been there as "a college campus built in the middle of a city park."

The transfer means a drop in custody for

me from max to medium. Expect the unexpected! There has got to be a catch.

April – OMITTED

May – OMITTED

June, Tuesday, the 19th: Haven't heard anymore about being transferred. No doubt it will happen., and it is probably nothing more ominous than D__ deciding to get rid of me.

July – OMITTED

August, Wednesday, the 15th, packing day. I never expected to leave here alive and in one piece. I haven't much to take with me; my typewriter, my second -- wore out the first with six years of constant use. Mark bought this one; -- the television, a reading lamp and a crock-pot are all the appliances I have. The rest of the stuff, with the exception of my dictionaries and toiletries, I can replace or live without, except for my writings, which are voluminous and fill a large cardboard box. Even the loss of one page could be a disaster. The same is true of my legal briefs and court opinions rejecting my constant appeal;, but of what use are appeals in a court system dominated by U.S. Supreme Court Judges who act more like mindless clerks, subverting the law to their clerks' duties? In any case, all I can do is pack and turn the documents over to the guards for shipping, hoping nothing is lost in transit.

I haven't heard of anyone leaving with me, but unless I know him, I wouldn't. There are over 2,000 inmates imprisoned here. I would be surprised if I'm the only one leaving. There is also a long waiting list of eighteen months to two years for the institution where I'm going. Why someone with my knowledge, and views of the system would be jumped to the head of the list, or even considered for transfer to a medium security institution, puzzles me, but no sense worrying. At worse, all it can mean is a round trip ticket, and if truth be told, I have adapted just a little too well to a prison that is known as "America's 48 Bloodiest Acres."

At this point, I'll take the happy ending.